NO TRACE

NO TRACE

JIM CRIGLER

A MASON & PENFIELD MYSTERY

BOOK 3

Cover design by Rey Ortiz deadidlemedia@gmail.com

ISBN 979-8-9992595-1-6

Wednesday, June 20

The Handler was parked fifty or sixty yards down the road from the entrance, far enough away that the camera that covered the entrance wouldn't see him. And he was here in a rental car sporting a stolen license tag. He would only use the tag once, but that was all he intended. He was here to do preliminary scouting for his backup plan.

From the outside, the warehouse park was as boring as a set of concrete-block buildings could be. Maybe its chain link fence was twice as high as most; maybe there was a second fence, just as high, inside the first; maybe both were topped with coils of razor concertina wire; maybe lights never turned off between the fences; maybe there were motion detectors and cameras constantly watching the area between; maybe, if you looked even closer, you'd see more concertina wire woven all through both fences.

Maybe if you knew where to look, near the woods on the back side, three closely spaced trees, outside, between, and

1

inside the fences had grown back from their stumps to three or four feet high; but they were so covered with kudzu that the insidious, broad leaves shielded the stumps from the view of the cameras, and the mound of kudzu could have hidden a tunnel through both fences, and would in fact do so if the backup plan was needed.

The Handler knew where to look. He had been inside the fences, inside one of the three warehouses only once, and that was more than six years ago. He knew what was being protected behind all that security. He had once been close to acquiring it, had held The Box *in his own hands*. And he had handed The Box, unopened, to someone who had no clue. His government — his *adopted* government — would use the knowledge there, or, if it was unable to use it directly, sell it for hard currency to someone who could.

His asset was in place and would provide adequate cover when he needed it. Ironically, the asset worked with the man the Handler had handed The Box to.

His deadline was approaching; if reassigned, he would be in the new place by People's Unity Day. If not reassigned, he would still be in America, but on the run. He knew the alternative to reassignment.

If tonight's interaction with the Brain — the primary plan — didn't get him what he needed, or at least start the process, the backup plan would be in place. One way or another, the Handler's business with the Brain would be finalized tonight.

11:38 p.m.

Tonight Ron Penfield couldn't sleep. Again.

At dinner he had yelled at everyone, including his daughter, Elena, who was universally called Lenna. And it hadn't even been *about* anything, just that her napkin had dropped from her lap to the floor. Who cared about that? Ron would have to apologize in the morning.

Lenna had tried to leave the table, but Ron had cowed her back into her chair, had commanded her to eat the rest of her dinner, which she had somehow choked down. But when she left the table, she retreated to her bedroom for about a minute before she ran to the bathroom to throw up. After that, she locked herself in her room and sobbed herself to sleep.

If only Lenna didn't look so much like Barb. The guilty feeling made it hard for Ron to breathe.

Ron's younger son, Edward — they used to call him Bumper, but now he asked to be called Ed — Ron had had enough of his smart mouth. He had been named after Ron's brother, which, given his wisecracking, was appropriate. And that was another reminder Ron didn't want. Ed (the older one) was a lush, even if he was mostly managing to hold his law practice together. Unlike his marriage.

When Ron was bulldozing over Lenna, Ronny — Ron Jr — nearly came out of his chair, fists clenched, face flushed. When his sister's napkin fell, Ron Jr had been describing his prospects of starting at first base on his college baseball team when Ron exploded. Ron had slapped him verbally, too, deprecating his "sportsball."

Everyone had just fallen silent rather than endure more

3

bullying from their father. The only sound heard for the last few minutes of dinner was feet shuffling to the sink to scrape dishes and add them to the dishwasher.

After sitting alone, fuming, Ron had eventually followed suit, then started the dishwasher and retreated to his home office. He sat in subdued gloom until around eleven o'clock, when he went to toss and turn hoping for sleep that was too intimidated by his verbal savagery to approach.

Gloria, Ron's mother-in-law, had been out for dinner with a friend, and she had missed the detonation, coming in after Lenna cried herself to sleep.

Thursday, June 21

I wonder, Ruthie Sellers thought, *whether Book would like a surprise visit.* She had finished her late shift at Chaps & Spurs, but Janae (that was Anabelle's real name) had asked her to swap closing nights and was finishing the stragglers tonight. So, Ruthie had extra time tonight — *this morning, really,* she thought. Besides, her shift tomorrow — *tonight now,* she thought — didn't start until six fifteen, so she could sleep all day if she needed to. After she went home. Maybe one day she could just stay ...

Ruthie decided to make the drive. If Nathan Bookman's lights were all off, she could just drive by and go on home. So instead of the normal late-night drive on surface streets, she directed her old Mazda 3 over to State Highway 400 for the trip "up north". Ruthie would sometimes call Book a Yankee for living on the north side of Atlanta. He'd shake his head in mock anger and revert to his native LA dialect — in his case,

LA meant *Lower Alabama.* Thinking of that made her smile as she took the only Bristow exit.

Turning onto Book's street and following the curve around to the left, Ruthie saw tail lights of a car moving away. She thought the dual stacked tail lights and brake light segments outside and smaller backup lights inboard reminded her of a car one of the boys (*he really* was *a boy*) from her high school had driven. Was that old muscle car a Dodge? She couldn't tell. The car disappeared around a curve to the right.

A house or two before Book's, which was on the left, Ruthie saw a dim light blink in a window on the right. *Someone must be up late.*

She slowed to a crawl in front of Book's house and looked, but there wasn't a hint of light crossing the lawn that she could see. As she sped up, following the now-disappeared tail lights, she thought, *Oh well. I'll need to let him know I am closing for Janae tonight, so I'll be later than usual.* Maybe *that* would be a night she got to stay.

Ruthie ignored the nagging whisper that tonight was someone else's night.

7:34 a.m.

Clarissa Miller peeked through the window in the door between the Penfields' garage and kitchen. She could see the youngest Penfield, Ed, hunched over a bowl of cereal. She also saw a shadow on the floor that suggested someone moving around in the kitchen, but since she couldn't see who it was, she rapped lightly with a knuckle.

Ron Penfield appeared in the window and smiled when he

saw her. *That* was something she would like to see more of, though right now Ron's bloodshot eyes obscured the effect.

Ron opened the door and said, "Hi! Come on in."

Clarissa winced slightly as she stepped up into the kitchen. That pain in her abdomen was coming more and more often, but it subsided on the level floor of the kitchen.

"Is Gloria not here?" she asked.

"Afraid not," Ron said.

Since the death of Barbara, Ron's wife and Gloria's daughter, Gloria split her time between the Penfields' house and her own home in Houston, Texas.

Clarissa's face was arrested in its fall when Ron continued, "Lenna drove her to the store for something. I think it was as much to give Lenna practice driving as anything else. They should be back in a few minutes."

Lenna, Clarissa knew, had just received her driving permit.

Ron spoke to his younger son. "Say hello, Ed."

"Hello, Ed," came croaking from behind the cereal box on the table.

Clarissa replied hello, and Ron said, "Would you like coffee? It's a fresh pot, and one of my favorite varieties."

"No, thanks. I was going to have tea with Gloria. I'll come back over later on." She turned back toward the door. Ed got up and took his dishes to the sink, then shuffled off toward the back stairs.

"No, no!" Ron said, "They'll only be a few more minutes. Just wait here."

"If you don't mind ..."

"It's perfectly okay. Let me pour some coffee and we can talk until they get back."

As she sat at the table, across the corner from the seat Ed

7

had just vacated, Ron turned back to retrieve and fill a mug for himself. As he poured, Clarissa looked around the kitchen and saw that there were no changes, none at all, in the fourteen months since Barbara's death in a car wreck. The oak cabinets, the tiled countertops, even the paint were all just as Barbara had left them. Everything was immaculate, but ... frozen. Even the aroma of freshly-brewed coffee was exactly what she would have expected.

Ron sat in the chair Ed had abandoned. He must have seen her looking around the room, because he closed his eyes and gripped his pursed lips between his teeth.

The moment passed, and Ron asked, "How is work in the call center? Is that what you call it?"

Clarissa said, "Inside, yes. To folks who don't work there, that sounds too much like telemarketing, so outside it's 'emergency response center.'" Clarissa worked for the county as a nine-one-one operator.

As Ron took his first sip, she thought, *How can something that smells so good taste so awful?*

"You've worked there several years."

"I've been able to work there longer than a lot of people."

"Why, do you think?"

Clarissa considered that for a minute. "I think it's because I had to become detached emotionally, dealing with my mother's drinking after my father left us. I had to be the adult. Which is tough when you're fourteen."

"I wish," Ron said, "I could get you to talk to a couple of the students at Armstrong about that. They're in a similar situation, thinking of dropping out of school from the pressure. Can I ask? What kept you with your mother, kept you going, kept you from chucking it all and going on your own?"

She put off answering by saying, "You ask hard questions." After a moment, she answered. "I think it was knowing the time was limited. I went to summer school and graduated a year early and got myself admitted to college and moved out. I can count the number of times I've been home since then on two hands a couple of toes. And just one hand for the times that weren't holidays."

Ron nodded and fell silent for a minute. Then he asked a question she didn't want to answer, a question Gloria had asked a few months ago but had never come up between Ron and Clarissa.

"Did you take the call ...?" He didn't finish the question. Clarissa thought he couldn't. He took a sip from his mug; Clarissa thought he might be trying to hide his face, at least partially.

Clarissa shook her head *no*. "I was on duty, but someone else took the call." After a pause, she added, "I was so sorry when Barb was killed. After Abe left and took all our friends, Barb was the only real friend I had. It was ..."

Silence fell and they sat awkwardly for a few moments.

Clarissa finally said, "I should be going. I can come back when Gloria's here."

She stood and took a couple of steps. Suddenly feeling a sharp pain in her side, she stumbled. Ron sprang from his chair and caught her arm to keep her from falling, then circled her slowly her back to her chair.

His brow furrowed with concern. "Do you need to see a doctor?"

She eased into her chair, and again shook her head *no*. "It ... will pass. It just takes a little while." She felt almost out of breath. "You should ... go on to work. Gloria told me you

9

... still have ... summer hours."

Ron glanced at the clock on the oven control panel. He thought for a moment, then said "No" and fished in his pocket for his cell phone. Selecting a number from his contacts, he placed a call.

"Constance, this is Ron Penfield. Can you check my calendar? ... Do I have anything before nine fifteen or so? ... Okay, when he comes in, can you ask to reschedule? ... Any vacant slot today after nine forty-five or tomorrow is fine. Tell him I'm sorry, but something urgent came up. Thanks a lot."

Clarissa had recovered a little of her breath, and she said, "I shouldn't keep you. Besides, I have to be at work at nine."

"That's *not* a good idea," Ron said. "If this is some kind of recurring thing, you should see a doctor as soon as you can."

"Really, no," Clarissa protested.

"Let me make a pot of tea. It will be ready when Gloria gets back, and it will help you relax some."

Fetching the copper kettle from the stove, he filled it with water and returned it to a burner, which he turned on full. He fetched the teapot and the infuser from the drain board and set them next to the range.

Looking in the cabinet, he asked, "Which tea would you like?"

"Really, I wish you wouldn't fuss. You can go on to work — I'll be all right."

Ron put on a look that seemed to say, *I'm a high school counselor; you can't fool me.* "And the answer to my question?"

Clarissa gave in. "If you're sure ... Could you make some of the Amazon Guayusa?"

"That's one of Gloria's favorites." Ron opened the cannister, then realized he didn't know proportions.

10

Seeing his uncertainty, Clarissa said, "Three level measures to a full pot of water."

Ron filled the infuser and attached its lid. "Does Gloria put the tea in before the water or after?"

"After. Then four minutes to steep."

Ron nodded and sat back down.

"Barb used to tell me how much she enjoyed talking with you."

"When I wasn't complaining, you mean."

He snorted lightly. "She said you had a lot to complain about."

"How much did she tell you?"

"Not much."

Clarissa looked at the stove as the kettle entered the noisy phase of heating. She wasn't sure she believed him — Ron and Barbara had been married, after all.

"Seriously," he assured her. "Your secrets were safe with her."

They sat quietly for a couple of minutes until the kettle began to whistle. Ron crossed to the stove, turned off the burner, and decanted the water into the teapot. Then he gently lowered the infuser into the water. The infuser was on a chain with a hook at the other end, which he affixed to the lip of the pot, then set the lid on.

As he returned to the table with the steeping tea, Ron asked, "What do you take in your tea?"

"Just some honey."

"Cup or mug?"

"A mug, please."

He fetched a mug, a spoon, and a jar of honey to the table. Ron was about to sit back down when they both heard a car park in the garage. Ron stayed on his feet as the car shut off, and a moment later, Gloria entered, dressed in navy slacks and a coral-colored cotton blouse.

As Gloria smiled and apologized for not being home on time, Lenna followed carrying grocery bags.

About to wave off Gloria's apology, Clarissa caught her breath, almost gasping.

As Lenna passed through the shadow by the door, Clarissa wanted to rush to her and hug her — from the mental cloud of her pain, she almost thought Lenna was Barbara: her height, her hair color, the way she carried herself, and, as Lenna emerged from the shadow, the shape and color of her eyes and the shape of her nose — all of it made her think of her friend.

Clarissa blinked away the beginning of tears and smiled.

Ron made a point of telling Gloria about Clarissa's pain episode, then left for work.

Clarissa and Gloria sat and talked and drank their tea while Lenna put the groceries away. And if Clarissa's gaze lingered a moment on Ron as he left, well, she was grateful for his kindness and his putting off work to make sure she was okay.

At least, gratitude was what she told herself.

9:46 a.m.

"Tell me what you see, Alcalá." Detective John Mason spoke to his new protégé as they drove up to the crime scene.

Two patrol cars and a UPS truck sat at the curb; one uniformed police officer stood halfway up the walk, keeping unauthorized people outside the perimeter and off the drive-way while another staked the lawn and ran crime scene tape a foot or so short of the sidewalk that ran down the street.

This was Mark Alcalá's first plain-clothes case since finishing his classroom work. Before he had a chance to answer, the medical examiner's truck pulled up behind the Crime Scene van, which was in front of the house next door; neither blocked the driveway. The personnel exited their vehicles, carrying their initial equipment.

"Well," Alcalá drew the word out about two seconds, eyes half closed, seeming to concentrate on the end of his long, straight nose. He started ticking off particulars in his Upper Northwest, nasal drawl.

"Looks like a normal suburban house. The yard is well kept, but nothing special — just grass and a little shrubbery and a border. The house won't need a roof or paint for a few years. There's no evidence of a pet, but the victim may keep — may have kept, I mean — any pets inside or out back. A few small spots on the driveway indicate at least one car parked there occasionally, but it could have been the owner. As we drove up, I saw a six-foot privacy fence. Blinds in the first-floor windows are the ordinary two-inch plantation type, and they're all closed; but the big picture window appears to have sheers and drapes. Second floor has the same type of blinds mostly, except for the window above the garage, which has a shade."

"Not bad," Mason said, opening the car door. "Now tell me what you don't see."

Alcalá blinked as they approached the sidewalk that led to the front door.

"Huh? How can I tell you what I don't see unless I've seen it before and know it's missing? Assuming you don't want something absurd, like a flying saucer. There's a garage, and we don't really have public transportation here, so he probably has a car in there."

Both detectives showed their IDs to the officer watching the perimeter, who logged their entry in a small notebook. He knew them — the Bristow police force wasn't big — but he needed their badge numbers.

As he returned his badge holder to his belt, Mason asked, "Do you follow cars — sports cars, NASCAR, Indy, any of that?

"No, sir, though I do like to look at new pickup trucks at the dealer when I get a chance. Then the sticker reminds me why I'm just looking."

Mason nodded.

"Why'd you ask that, sir?"

"Leave 'sir' to the uniforms. It's 'John' or 'Mason' or 'Detective.' I asked about cars because if you're *not* a big fan, it'll help you be objective when we get inside."

Alcalá's eyebrows rose, and his head tilted, but he didn't say anything. He just followed Mason up the walk.

Alcalá asked, "How was the body found?"

"The delivery driver has a package that requires a signature, looks down through the blind to the right of the front door, sees legs, calls nine-one-one. Patrol officer opens the front door, which was unlocked, finds the body. The body is cool and has no pulse, so she calls it in as a suspicious death. More patrol officers are called to protect the scene, then forensics, the M.E. and us. I got the initial brief from Officer Caligari over the phone."

"Not a heart attack or stroke?"

"Didn't I mention? Caligari also said he has a hole in his forehead."

Both detectives put on gloves and stood outside the front

door.

Mason called through the open door, "Are we set yet, Maddie?"

Madeline Welch, the CSU forensics lead, called back, "A couple of minutes, Detective. Foot coverings and gloves should be there by the door."

"Is Caligari in there?"

"I think she's in the kitchen, John. Do you want her out there?"

"Yes, please."

They heard Welch call for the uniformed officer.

Caligari came through the living room, skirting the center of the room, properly gloved and shoes covered. Tall and athletic, with a solid torso discernable through her uniform and light body armor, Catherine Caligari approached the front door with a slightly crooked smile beneath East Asian eyes and a layer of Vick's under her Mediterranean nose.

After a round of introductions, Mason said, "Walk us through your discovery."

"There's not much to it, Detective. I was dispatched out of a nine-one-one call made by the delivery driver. When I came up to the door, he explained why he called and had me look down through the slats of the blinds. The body was there. I tried the door and found it unlocked; checked for a pulse and found none, and the body had lost a lot of heat. I noticed the gunshot wound in his forehead and started making calls. The delivery guy had called for an ambulance, and the ambulance crew pronounced him dead at the scene and left."

Mason asked, "Did you get their names?"

"Yes, sir. Tannen and Valrico. Ambulance number K-C-M-one-zero."

"You've given your movements to the Crime Scene squad?"

"Not yet, sir," Caligari said. "They asked me to wait in the kitchen."

Alcalá said, "I saw the driver waiting in his truck. Did he enter the house?"

"No, sir. He waited on the front porch when I came in, then I asked him to wait in his truck for detectives — for you, sir." She nodded to Mason.

Mason returned the nod. "Search of the house?"

"When backup arrived, two of us did a thorough search. There was no one here."

"Did you find a weapon?"

"None, sir."

Mason drew part of a breath through his teeth. "Okay. After you've given your movements to Forensics, bring the driver to the porch, then assemble four officers as a canvassing unit and wait for instructions from one of us." Mason indicated himself and Alcalá.

Mason and Alcalá donned foot coverings as Caligari went to comply. Since they had a few more seconds, Mason said, "What do you see around the door?"

Alcalá examined the door, concentrating on the opening lever and the lock.

"There are some minor scratches around the lock. Can't tell about fingerprints."

"Do you think anyone tampered with it?"

"Can't tell for certain." He inhaled deeply for a second. "Wouldn't someone picking the lock be more careful, though? Trying hard to leave no trace?"

Before they stepped into the house, Mason asked, "When

you were in uniform, were you ever at a scene with a body?"

Alcalá shook his head.

"You'll want some of these, then."

Mason handed Alcalá a few small items wrapped in candy paper.

"I make these myself to get them strong enough," Mason said.

Welch called out, "Okay, John, you can come in now."

When they entered the living room, the reason for the mints was obvious. Decay of the corpse was not far advanced, but the spilling of bodily fluids at death resulted in an oppressive stench.

Mason opened a mint and popped it in his mouth, and Alcalá did the same. His nose and throat were immediately overmastered with peppermint.

The detectives stepped inside onto a hardwood floor. Mason asked, "What kind of perimeter do we have?"

"Six feet for now. You want the usual radial clearance?"

Mason nodded. "Yes, and make sure the lock on the front door is early on the list."

"Always is." She turned to the other tech. "Guarneri, go do the front door and all that."

Guarneri nodded and said, "And pay attention to the dead-bolt. Got it." He stepped around the detectives and outside, then pulled the door almost closed.

Mason looked at Alcalá, whose face was drawn as he sucked violently on the hard candy.

Glancing around the body, Mason saw discoloration on the floor where the victim's urine had spilled post mortem, then evaporated; the pants were soiled from his feces on the back.

Turning to Mason, Welch smiled and said, "Who's the new

17

guy?"

Mason introduced her to Alcalá, then said, "Now, Maddie, watch this. Mark, describe this room."

"All right." Alcalá extended *right* for a couple of seconds as his eyelids lowered halfway.

"This is a formal living room. It has a hardwood floor, probably bamboo, over a concrete slab. Walls are greyed-out vermilion. The room is about twelve feet by fourteen, and the center of the floor is covered by a Turkish rug that's six and a half by nine and a half, give or take. The furniture is chrome and black leather, which is unusual with the rug, but it works because the rug has a lot of black in it. The coffee table and end tables have glass tops with beveled edges and just a chrome frame underneath, so you can see through to the floor."

Mason asked, "What's your impression of the style?"

"It looks Euro-modern, but designer, not IKEA."

"The pictures?"

Alcalá paused a second and said, "Black and white photography of the Carina nebula, split into a four-by-two grid in twenty-inch square frames, with some space between pictures, sort of a 'window on the universe' effect."

"That's pretty specific," Welch said. "How do you know what the subject is?"

"You can download the pictures from hubblesite.org, and someone followed the framing suggestion there."

"Pickup trucks and stars, huh?" Mason muttered. "What else have you got under the hood?" He turned to Welch. "Who's your new guy?"

"Name's Roberto Guarneri. He's been warned." She turned to resume examining the rest of the room.

The detectives kneeled to start their look over the body.

18

"Warned?" Alcalá said.

"Only the leads for forensics and the medical examiner get to call us by our first names. To everyone else it's 'Detective Mason' and 'Detective Alcalá'."

Alcalá nodded and filed that away for the future. "Should I tell you what I see on the body?"

Mason smiled and said, "Naw, I'll take a turn. You can write it all down."

The body lay on its left side on the hardwood, back to the door, leaning slightly over toward the front. The thighs extended at an angle, the right at a greater angle than the left, both calves at right angles to their thighs. The torso trapped the left upper arm, leaving the forearm at almost a right angle; the right arm was straight and pointed at the left foot.

Mason blinked a couple of times and started talking, fast.

"The victim is a white male, about five feet, seven inches, roughly one hundred fifty pounds. Curly hair that falls to the base of his neck, but if you called it a 'mullet,' he'd start a fight, especially after a couple of drinks. He's wearing lightweight long pants, likely pajama pants, and a T-shirt that has a logo from ..." Mason craned his upper body around to see. "Shirt's from Cal Tech."

Alcalá kept scribbling, and when he caught up, his eyebrows went down, and he looked up. "You said 'start a fight'." He popped another mint. "Did you know this guy?"

Mason said, "Yeah, we worked together a long time ago. Name's Nathan Bookman."

He pointed to the victim's forehead. "Look here. Looks like a small caliber round, single shot, no visible residue, just a single trickle of blood that didn't even reach the floor. No exit wound. The ME and forensics will be able to tell us more."

When Mason picked up the right hand, the torso rotated slightly. He looked all around the arm. "Full or near-full *rigor mortis.* Nothing on the right arm indicates a struggle. I'm going to let the Medical Examiner's people move the body before I look at the left arm, but the part I can see is similarly unmarked."

Guarneri came back inside, and Welch pointed him to the place he should start on the room.

Mason pulled the shirt away from the body at the waist and looked up it at the torso using a small flashlight. "No cuts or bruising are visible on the torso, but the ME will tell us about that later. Call them in."

The Medical Examiner's people came in and started their preliminary check.

Mason tapped with a thumb against the base knuckles on his opposite hand.

"John," Welch said, "What's your priority when we finish this room?"

Mason suppressed a grin. "Give me a path to the garage and clear the garage. But don't say anything about what you find there. I want Alcalá here to see it cold."

"Okay, no problem. You got that, Roberto?"

"Sure do, Maddie. Cold and frozen."

"Normal drill on the body," Mason said. "After that, do the rest of the house in whatever order makes sense.

Welch nodded.

"Mark, you watch things in here," Mason said. "Leave everyone plenty of room to work, but see what they see."

Alcalá nodded and took up a position three or four feet behind Guarneri. Mason went outside.

"Got anything so far?" Alcalá asked.

"Just some hair, same color as the vic's," Guarneri said. "I checked the window sill for fingerprints, but there weren't any, consistent with someone dusting after the windows were last handled. The furniture is dusted and polished regularly, and there are a few prints there, but I'd be surprised if they don't belong to the victim."

"Roberto!" Welch said. "You are *not! not! not!* to do *any kind* of guesswork. We deal with evidence *only*. Facts. No suppositions."

Guarneri stood, upright and wide-eyed, and said "Yes, ma'am." When he saw Welch continue working, he got back to work as well.

"Ms Welch," Alcalá said, "What did John mean about 'normal drill on the body' a few minutes ago?"

"The ME's guys are waiting until Roberto and I are finished with this room before moving the body. We won't touch the body, but we'll supervise the lifting, get and log any evidence trapped underneath, and so on."

"Did you photograph the room yet?"

Welch rolled her eyes. "Don't insult me, Mark. Photos first, then physical — you should know that."

Outside, Mason organized the canvassing of the neighborhood. Two officers in plain clothes and two in uniform, including Caligari, got their instructions to go door-to-door, finding out whether anyone on this block or the one behind had heard, seen or suspected anything surrounding the victim or his house. Two more forensics techs were examining the yard, the driveway, and the sidewalk.

Mason talked to the UPS driver, whose story matched what he already told Officer Caligari. After making sure they had possession of the package he was delivering and a copy of his fingerprints for elimination, Mason let him go.

When Mason was satisfied with the arrangements around the outside of the house, he went back in.

The ME lead, a heavyset woman whose name tag read 'F. Plasse', said, "John, if all else is equal — air temp steady in the mid-seventies, no drugs or medical weirdness, no trauma prior to the apparent gunshot wound — the victim died at least eight hours ago, but not more than fourteen."

"So roughly between eight p.m. and two a.m."

"Yep."

Welch and Guarneri completed their sweep of the room, so they and the detectives gathered around the body. When Plasse and her assistant had it off the ground, Welch photographed the floor and the underside of the body; Guarneri ran the lint collection; Mason checked the victim's left side and left arm for cuts and bruises, finding only *livor mortis*, the settling of blood to the bottom.

"Gravity still works," he muttered.

While Plasse and her coworker loaded the body onto a gurney, Mason told Alcalá, "You go check with the canvassing officers on this block and the block behind, then come back here."

Alcalá nodded and headed out, followed by the body of Nathan Bookman.

The outside forensics techs came to the door, put on booties, and came inside. The doorway to the kitchen had already been cleared by Welch, so she told them to work the path to the door to the garage, followed by the rest of the kitchen.

Welch said, "Why the hush-hush on the garage, John?"

"Just what I told you, Maddie, I want Mark to see the garage cold."

"Okay, your call."

Welch shook her head and stood at the entry to the kitchen for a couple of minutes while the two techs finished the path to the garage door. They cleared it just as Guarneri finished his side of the living room and came up.

Welch and Guarneri opened the door of the garage, got prints from the light switch, and turned on the garage light.

They stood still and upright for a full minute, stunned.

Mason watched them from an angle, grinning.

Welch called the other two forensics techs to get a look. One drew up, mouth open; the other just shrugged and went back to his work.

Taking the cue, the other three resumed their work as well.

A few minutes later, Mark Alcalá returned.

"John, I think you should go talk to the gatekeeper."

"How come?"

"There are two suits demanding access to the scene."

"Weird," Mason said as he crossed the living room to the front door. He turned around and called back, "Go have a look in the garage now."

Alcalá went through the kitchen and stood at the door to the garage. He looked through the door as Welch and Guarneri continued to work.

He saw a red DeTomaso Pantera, small and raked body, with a high spoiler painted black; and a dark gray Lamborghini Gallardo Spyder, with the muscular body that Corvette designers had never quite achieved. The Spyder's top was down, revealing white leather upholstery.

"Whoa." Alcalá stood staring with his mouth open.

He stepped into the garage, but stepped back when Guarneri said, "Not yet Detective. You can stand inside the door and look, but stay put until we finish."

Welch nodded and added, "If we find something we think you'll want to see right away, we'll call you over."

Alcalá stood still and started breathing again.

———————

Outside, Mason sized up the two suits as he approached the perimeter. One wore gray with a blue and red striped tie, the other wore black with a black tie.

Mason asked the uniformed officer controlling the perimeter, "Everything okay, Stanton?"

Stanton nodded and said, "Yes, detective. These gentlemen are cooperating, but they would like to talk to you."

Mason peeled off his glove and offered a hand. "John Mason, detective in charge of the crime scene."

The man closer to Mason, the one with the striped tie, shook Mason's hand. "This is Robert Grove, and I'm Victor Orozco, FBI."

Grove also shook Mason's hand.

"Why do you want access to our crime scene?"

Orozco asked, "Was the owner of the house, Nathan Bookman, the perpetrator or perhaps the victim here?"

"He was the victim. Again, why does this purely local matter interest the Bureau?"

Grove nodded to Orozco, who said, "Mr Bookman was the subject of an ongoing investigation. That's all I can tell you right now."

Mason closed his eyes for a second and said, "Okay, I can allow you access as guests, but if you don't observe our crime scene protocol in detail, you will have to leave." *Or be removed,* he thought. *But it probably won't come to that.*

Orozco raised an eyebrow and Grove nodded.

"Shouldn't be a problem," Orozco said.

The two men started up the walk.

"Hold it!" Mason said. "Rule number one is you present your credentials to the officer acting as gatekeeper. He logs all access to the scene."

In turn, the men showed IDs to Stanton, who noted names and badge numbers along with the FBI designation, then both headed up the walk, Mason following.

Mason asked, "So, what can you tell me about your interest in Bookman's death?"

Grove said, "We can't talk about it right now. Sorry. We still have a live investigation."

These were the first words Mason had heard from Grove, and Mason hid his surprise at hearing him speak.

"Okay," Mason said as they reached the door. "Wait here."

Mason disappeared inside the house for a minute, and reappeared with gloves and foot coverings, which had been moved inside. As the agents were putting them on, Mason said, "The body has already been removed, and our forensics techs are going over the house. Is either of you a car aficionado?"

Both agents shook their heads.

Mason thought, *You may turn into one after today.*

Orozco said, "What can you tell us about the body?"

"It was found lying on the floor a few feet inside the front door, which was unlocked. Preliminary examination showed the victim was probably dead ten to twelve hours, give or take."

They stepped inside, and Mason said, "You can look in this room, the kitchen and the garage. More will be available as the forensics folks clear it."

As Orozco asked, "How did he die?", Grove tapped his foot a couple of times on the hardwood floor and moved around to face Mason.

Mason said, "A single gunshot wound to the head. Again, everything's preliminary until the experts weigh in, but that's how it looks right now."

"Any signs of a struggle?"

"Nothing obvious on the body, and no disruption of the house. Also, there are no obvious signs of forced entry."

"Consistent with an unlocked door."

"Not inconsistent with it, anyhow."

Welch looked through from the kitchen. "John, we've finished with the dining room, the kitchen, the half-bath and the hallway. Roberto and I are still working in the garage, but you know what a mess they can be."

Mason said, "Sure," and he introduced Welch to the agents.

Grove tapped his foot a couple of times and moved toward the kitchen door.

Orozco said to Welch, "Is there a way we can get a copy of your report when it's available?"

"That's up to Detective Mason, but my department has no problem with it."

Mason said, "It shouldn't be a problem. I'll get my lieutenant started on the paperwork. Can I have an address or something to send it to?"

Orozco handed Mason a business card from his wallet, and Mason walked into the kitchen, fishing his cell phone from his pocket.

As he dialed, Alcalá motioned from the garage for Mason to step in. Mason smiled as he spoke to his lieutenant to plan for investigation results to be made available to FBI agent Orozco periodically.

After Mason rang off, Alcalá asked, "FBI? Why are they here?"

Mason told him what Grove said, then said, "Go introduce yourself to them and keep them in the living room for at least sixty seconds."

Mark nodded assent and went back through the kitchen.

Mason said, "Maddie, got a second?"

"Sure. What do you need?"

"After the FBI agents leave, I want you to take soundings of every square foot of every floor, every wall, every ceiling in the house. Go through the attic, too. Put your findings in an addendum report — call it an appendix or whatever — and don't reference it in the initial draft, not even the table of contents.

"What am I looking for?"

"Hiding places. If you find one, don't open it, just put it in the addendum."

"This will take overtime."

"Authorized. I'll tell you why later. Now I better let the fibbies out of the living room."

10:06 a.m.

Henery Guyée stood in front of a rack of white plastic pipes of various sizes in the hardware store. It was a small store, with some faucets and a couple of toilets in boxes farther down the row and toilet repair hardware behind him; electrical parts were just one aisle over, and nuts and bolts one aisle in the other direction. He only needed a foot-long piece of pipe and a cap, plus some hardware, for the project he had in mind. *Thin-walled or schedule 40?* Thin wall would be good enough — the rest of the structure would provide enough support.

A little below average height, Guyée was muscular, and his shaved head reflected the light from the skylights and the fluorescents overhead. The lights couldn't wash out the color of the deeply tanned skin and powerful arms and shoulders that indicated that he worked outdoors. He wore painter's pants and a work shirt; both were spattered with paint.

He heard steps coming toward him, and after a moment a man rounded the corner and came toward him. The man stopped in his tracks.

"Eight-ball!" the man said. "Is that you?"

"Mister Penfield? It *is* me!" His accent reflected his up-bringing in working-class New Orleans. His lips parted in a smile, revealing blinding white teeth.

Ron smiled and stuck out a hand. "How long has it been? Seven years? Eight?"

"Tha's about right. I was so sorry to hear about your wife last year." Eight-ball referred to the murder of Ron's wife by one of his students.

Ron nodded and the corners of his mouth pinched together. "Thanks. We're still living with it. At least the trial is over."

"I read about it. Wanted that girl to get more hard time than she got. But like you said, at least it's over. Where are you workin' now?"

"I'm the counselor at Armstrong High School."

"And your kids?"

"Ron Jr just finished his first year at Newman; Elena is a sophomore — rather, about to be a junior at Armstrong; Ed will be in eighth grade at Anthony Middle. What about you? What about that little gal you were seeing, the pretty Latina?"

"Let's see ... that long ago you must be talking about Rosa. Her mother didn't like me." His demeanor darkened, and his voice dropped in pitch as he went on. "She said Rosa has to marry Cath'lic. She say somebody who gave up on church is no good. She say come back when a priest will give me the sac'ament."

"And Rosa?"

"Rosa cried and cried," Eight-ball said. "But she did what her mamá *told* her to do." He closed his eyes for a moment.

Ron nodded. "Anyone steady since then?"

"Nobody who wanted to call home," Eight-ball said with a wink. "That's enough of that. What are you here for?"

"I have to replace some of the pipes for the sprinkler system. You?"

"Just need a piece of pipe and some hardware."

They chatted more as Ron selected pipe, cleaner, adhesive, and a couple of fittings, then Ron headed for the cashier as Guyée moved over to the hardware aisle.

Ron checked out and said goodbye to Guyée, who was entering the checkout line with a pipe and some fittings, and bags of metal washers and rubber washers.

12:18 p.m.

At home, Ron dug with a shovel in his side yard, just by the house. His younger son, Ed, was helping him, though not by choice.

"Here's the deal," Ron said. "The pipe runs underground,

29

and there's a T-joint and a vertical pipe coming up out of it for each sprinkler. If the vertical pipe has enough left below the break, we'll just trim it, clean it off, and attach a straight-line coupler to bring up the vertical pipe to the head. But if it's broken off too short, we'll have to cut the underground pipe and splice in a new piece with a new T-joint at one end."

Ed nodded as he unscrewed the cap of one of the small cans. "That solvent smells ugly."

"That's the cleaner, and it evaporates quickly, so we keep the top off the shortest time we can."

"Do we use this rag to put it on and get it off?"

"Just to wipe it off. There's an applicator attached to the underside of the lid."

"Why do *I* need to do this?"

"Two reasons," Ron said. "First, you broke it mowing the grass, so you have to learn to fix it."

"And second?"

"Second, if you break any more, you'll have to fix them by yourself. This way you learn a useful skill *and* learn to be more careful."

"And this plastic pipe is good enough for this?"

"Yep. It's called polyvinyl chloride, usually abbreviated PVC."

"Wait ..." Ed said. "Haven't I heard about it that being used in clothes?"

Ron nodded. "There's a treatment you can do on the material to make it more flexible. One of the teachers at Armstrong has a fake letter jacket from Michigan State that has PVC sleeves with a surface texture that looks almost like leather. The kind used in plumbing is stiffer, durable, stands up to pressure and can take a fair amount of shock."

"Just not a lawn mower pushing it over."

"And cutting it."

The shovel tip hit the underground pipe, so Ron put the shovel aside. The two of them pulled dirt out of the hole with their hands and looked at the pipe. About two inches of vertical was still attached to the T-joint. The break was jagged and varied along half an inch or so of the pipe.

"You're in luck," Ron said. "It's a lot easier this way."

"Okay, what do I do?"

Ron handed Ed a tool. "This is a cutter made for PVC pipe."

Ed looked at it. A ratcheting grip held a curved rest for the pipe. When the halves of the grip were squeezed repeatedly, a sharp, steel blade moved inexorably toward the rest.

"Not a good place for a finger," Ed said drily.

"Like a lot of tools, it's useful when handled correctly and used for what it's made for, and bloody-awful dangerous otherwise. Put that down and look at this."

Ed took the coupling, just a two- or three-inch long sleeve of PVC that would fit on the outside of the pipes.

"Feel the inside," Ron said.

Ed complied. "There's a ridge that circles it in the middle."

"Tell me what that's for."

Ed thought and said, "When you slide the pipe in from one side, it keeps it from going all the way through so you can insert the pipe you're joining to it from the other side."

"Very good. Okay, here's the procedure: First, cut the pipe in the ground so the cut is level."

"And so it will go all the way to the stop in the coupler."

"Right. Next, run this cleaner around the outside, then wipe it off with the rag right away."

"Because the cleaner evaporates quickly."

"Right. It's largely acetone or something, and you don't want it mixing with the adhesive."

Ed cut the pipe. "Is that good enough? It's not perfectly level."

"For this application it will do," Ron said. "If it were inside the house, we'd make it better. Think for a minute and tell me what the next problem is."

"That's easy. When I cut off the other pipe, the total height will be shorter by an inch or two. This sprinkler head is a constant height above ground, so will it be tall enough?"

"Once again, very good. And the answer in this case is yes, an inch or so won't make a big difference. So, get the other piece, cut it level and clean it the way you did the first one."

Ed again went through the cutting and cleaning routine.

"Is it time for the adhesive now?"

"Yep. We'll do the piece in the ground first. Put some adhesive around the pipe, then ring a little bit around the inside of one end of the coupling, then put that end of the coupling down on the pipe."

"How does the adhesive work?"

"Essentially, it dissolves the pipe onto the coupling."

"The two become one. Like marriage. But it doesn't weaken it?"

"It may, but the extra thickness of the coupling takes care of that."

Ed spread the adhesive (which he thought smelled worse than the cleaner) as his father had told him, then pushed the coupling onto the pipe.

"Is this stuff used in plumbing a lot? A minute ago, you said something about inside plumbing. Is it safe?"

"It used to be. It's corrosion resistant, easily withstands any temperature that comes out of a water heater. It can withstand a fair amount of pressure, but it might burst if water freezes in it, and that's easy to prevent. The biggest problem is that after a few years it gets brittle, probably because of the chlorine in the water, and then it doesn't take much to break it."

"Now I do the same with the other pipe and the top half of the coupling?"

"You got it. Just be sure when you put the pipe on that the sprinkler is pointed the right way."

Ed finished the job, then they filled in the hole, pushed the mulch back around it, put everything away, and went inside to wash up.

1:02 p.m.

The FBI agents, Grove and Orozco, cooperated fully as they followed the detectives and forensics specialists through the house: They only went into areas cleared by forensics, and they were never ahead of the detectives in their examination of the house. More than one person noticed Grove's odd foot-tapping.

The pair didn't stay long. Seeming to have satisfied themselves that the work was being done well, they left, repeating to both Mason and Welch that they would be looking for the detailed forensics report.

1:37 p.m.

Only a few neighbors had anything to say about Nathan Bookman or his house. No one was home at six of the twenty houses, and there was a pretty good chance some of those families were on vacation. Teenagers but no adults were home at three; these would be visited later, and the houses where no one answered the door would be periodically followed up as well.

But at one house, two doors down and across the street from Bookman's, Officer Caligari rang the bell. After a moment, a young woman holding an infant came to the door. Two other children, both under age five, nipped at her heels.

"Can I help you?" Her accent revealed her origin somewhere in Long Island.

Caligari smiled and said, "Hello, I'm Officer Caligari. Is there a chance I could ask you a couple of questions?"

"I have a minute," the young woman said. "I need to get Philip and Angie put down for their naps. Maria won't take one any more. I'm sorry about the little ones, officer. They want to see the flashing lights from the police cars. What do you want to know?" After a second, she said, "I'm Gina Macchia."

Gina was about five feet tall, seemed to be around twenty-five, about Caligari's own age. Gina wore both engagement and wedding rings, had short, honey-blond hair and a slight build, fair skin and green eyes. She wore a T-shirt that was solid dark blue, faded jeans that were much lighter in color than the shirt, and black Vans.

"It's okay, Mrs Macchia," Caligari said, her eyes narrowing in good humor as she smiled. "My cousin has two little guys.

34

Anyway, the house all the lights are in front of — do you know anyone who lives there?"

"That's that bachelor's house, isn't it? Bookard? Bookman? Was that the name? — Maria! Go back to the kitchen!"

"Yes ma'am, his name was Nathan Bookman. He was found dead at home. We were wondering whether you saw anyone coming or going in the last couple of days."

Gina Macchia sucked on her lower lip for a moment. "Well, no, not in the last couple of days. But . . ."

"Yes ma'am? What is it?"

"In the last few weeks — Philip, get back in here! — since the baby came, I've been up at night with her, and looking out the window from my kitchen, I saw — Maria! — saw a car, not a big one, four doors, dark color, parked in his driveway. I saw it twice, once at two in the morning, the other time must have been about one-thirty. The first time, I saw someone come out of the house and drive away."

"Can you describe who it was?"

"Mar! — It was dark, and I can't be certain, but it seemed like it was a woman, at least — Philip! Don't throw that! — at least it was someone with a small build and big, long, mostly straight hair, dressed pretty skimpily."

"Assuming it was a woman, could you tell how tall she was?"

Gina worked her lip again for a couple of seconds. "At first, I thought she was tall, about your height. But when she came around the car, I could see she wore platforms, like four or five inches."

"So, she was about average height."

She nodded. "Yeah. Yeah, she was."

"Would you describe her as thin, medium build, any amount overweight?"

35

"Not remotely overweight. Thin through the stomach and hips, narrow shoulders, large bust."

"And her hair color?"

"I couldn't tell for sure because it was the middle of the night, but it wasn't platinum. It was dark but wasn't black."

Caligari caught her notes up. "You said she dressed — what was it?"

"Skimpy. Tight fitting shirt, bare midriff, just a cover over her bra if she had one on — she needed one — and a short, short, tight skirt. I could tell she wore hose because her legs — Ma-*ria!* — were almost black but her arms looked pale by comparison even in just the streetlight in the middle of the night."

"But you didn't see her or a car the last couple of nights?"

Gina shook her head no. "Last night, a car like that one drove past just as I was up with Angela."

"Why were you up?"

She nodded. "Angie has decided her feeding time is around one fifteen, so I'm up most nights. There was no car in the driveway and no one in the street. At that time of night, I'd notice anyone at all."

Caligari caught her notes up again. "Is there a chance I could get a look through the window you saw all this through? It will help me describe it to the detective."

"Well, okay." Gina didn't seem happy about her coming inside, but she nodded and led the way to the kitchen. "I hope you can stand the mess, but the older kids have kept me too busy to straighten up this morning."

"It's not a problem, ma'am." Caligari would have said that no matter the condition of the house. The only thing that seemed remotely out of place was a dish towel on the kitchen counter.

The kitchen garden window projected out from the house ten or twelve inches. Three small pots sat on either of two shelves; herbs grew in them, but they were not tall.

"Can you describe what you do when you get up to feed the baby?"

Gina nodded. "There's a night light over there" — she indicated the far wall — "so I don't need to turn a light on. Before feeding, I fix a cup of herbal tea, and after Angie is back in bed, I put the cup by the sink. That's what I was doing when I saw the woman. The other time, the time I just saw the car, was when I was making the tea."

Caligari noted that the angle from the left side of the sink allowed her (or would have, had all the official vehicles not been in the way) a good view of Nathan Bookman's driveway, which ran up to the garage on the near side of the house. A guest coming out the front door would be on the far side of her car and have to come around to drive away. Unless . . .

"When the car was parked there, it was pulled into the driveway?"

Gina nodded.

"Facing forward, not backed in?"

"Mm, hmm."

So Caligari's original idea was right: Gina Macchia would have a good view of the driver getting into or out of a car.

After thanking Gina and allowing her son to hold her flashlight for a moment, Caligari made a note, "RELIABLE WITNESS", then crossed the street and told Alcalá about Bookman's late-night visitor. Then she went on to the next house.

7:00 p.m.

The initial examination of Nathan Bookman's house turned up nothing. In fact, it turned up far too much nothing.

All the fingerprints found were from the same three pairs of hands; later comparison would show them to be the victim's and his two cleaning ladies. All the hair was the color and consistency of the victim's. Dirty clothes were found in a hamper next to a stack of drop-off bags from a local laundry; Mason knew the laundry was frequented by well-off people.

The only electronics in the house were a TV in a room best described as a home office, and another, very large TV mounted to the wall in the master bedroom. Of the two other bedrooms, one was set up as a home gym, the other as a guest room.

In his preliminary report, Mark Alcalá would write that Bookman appeared to live alone, to be habitually neat, and to seldom entertain. Of course, all this was based on examination and informal descriptions of the earliest trace evidence, all subject to change.

And some would be changed, based on another preliminary report Alcalá wouldn't see until the next day.

Friday, June 22

1:35 a.m.

Ruthy was exhausted after an extra-busy Thursday night at Chaps & Spurs. She called Book's cell phone and left a message that she wouldn't be there for their usual *tête-à-tête*. Out of energy as she was, she giggled, remembering the term Book used to use. She was just alert enough to safely wend her way to her efficiency apartment.

She didn't know she wouldn't be meeting him again.

8:00 a.m.

Mason rang the doorbell and waited. After a moment, Ron Penfield answered the door.

"Got a few minutes?" Mason asked.

"Sure," Ron replied. "Come on in." As they approached the kitchen, Ron said, "I haven't seen you since the trial." Both knew the only trial he could mean was the murder trial of Vicky

Winstead, who had killed Ron's wife, Barbara. "I have about half an hour before I need to get ready to go to the office."

"Abbreviated summer hours?"

Ron nodded.

"Wish I had those."

Mason said hello to Lenna, who was just finishing her breakfast.

"Is Gloria here?" Mason asked.

Ron shook his head as he got coffee mugs from the cabinet. "No, she left early with friends to go to Callaway Gardens. Bumper and Ronny — Ed and Ron Jr; still getting used to it — are still asleep. Speaking of which, it's early for you to be out and about," Ron said.

John nodded. "Have you seen the news?"

"Not yet. I was just about to turn it on when you got here. What should I look for?"

Lenna placed her cereal bowl and spoon into the dishwasher, waved goodbye to the detective, and trudged up the back staircase.

While he poured John's coffee, Ron asked again, "So what's in the news?"

"Nathan Bookman is dead."

"A shame," Ron said. "Was he ever implicated in that business with Senator Jamison last fall?"

"Nope. Except for a single, unverified sighting, he was never tied in. McAlister absolutely refused to name him as co-conspirator, accomplice, not event an acquaintance." As he accepted the mug from Ron, Mason noticed that the kitchen appeared identical to the way it had looked months ago, when the Jamison case was concluding.

"I'm sorry he's dead," Ron said, "but I haven't seen him in

years. You?"

"Nope."

"How did you find out?"

"I was at his house well into the evening yesterday. He was murdered."

Ron took a sip of his coffee. "That's why you were *there*. The surprise is your coming *here*. Why did you come to tell me in particular?"

"Because while I was at the crime scene, two guys from the FBI showed up."

"Why? Seems like a local homicide-type thing to me."

"They wouldn't say. It *could* have been connected to Jamison, but I think they would have told me if it were. That doesn't leave much except ..."

"Except for Kaiser," Ron finished. "Hmm."

Both men stared into their coffee cups for a moment. All three had worked at Kaiser Transceivers, a small defense contractor.

"You could've called," Ron said.

Mason shook his head. "I've got a feeling about this. The crime scene was unremarkable, but the Bureau guys were acting funny. Something's up, Ron."

Ron said, "I wonder if it's connected ..."

"... to his cars," they finished together, both smiling.

"Which one was your favorite?" Ron asked.

"The MG — the antique."

"Really? I had you figured as a Corvette guy."

"The Corvette he had was the wrong year. And the dark green MG convertible — *that* was a car."

"What did he have in his garage yesterday?"

"He had the DeTomaso —"

"— the same as last fall," Ron cut in.

John nodded. "He also had a Lam. Dark gray convertible with white leather interior. Classiest thing I ever saw. My new second, Mark Alcalá, nearly melted when he saw it."

"Not Renfroe anymore?"

"Michael's going solo on small-to-medium breaking and entering and some assault when there's not much doubt. He's running slightly ahead of average in bringing cases in."

They chatted for a couple of minutes about baseball, then John asked, "Can I borrow the phone? I left my cell phone in the car."

Ron blinked as he recognized something, then said, "Sure."

John placed a brief call to his wife using Ron's house phone. From the conversation, Ron surmised she was on her way to her office, an upscale residential real estate brokerage.

When John rang off, he said, "Ann says hi. Anyway, thanks for the coffee," emphasizing *coffee* slightly. "But I've got to go through all the reports from the crime scene: Forensics, see what the Medical Examiner has if they've gotten to it, compare everything to canvassing reports. I don't really know where this one is headed."

Ron said, "Yeah, seems strange. ... What does thinking about Kaiser remind me of? ... I remember: Guess who I saw yesterday."

Mason shook his head.

"Eight-ball."

"The janitor? Where'd you see him?"

"At the hardware store. We were both getting PVC pipe."

"How's he doing?"

"Seemed to be fine."

"He still seeing the little Latina? The one with the big curls and pencil skirts?"

Ron shook his head. "Nope, Henery Guyée wasn't Catholic enough for her mother."

John drank off the last of his coffee, and Ron walked him to the door. Ron noticed John had parked three houses down.

9:10 a.m.

When Mason reached the squad room, Mark Alcalá was buried in reports spread out around him.

"What stands out so far?" Mason asked.

"Two things," Alcalá said. "First, the general lack of forensic evidence. The preliminary report came through around a quarter to eight. There were no fingerprints except the victim's in the living room, and barely any more in the kitchen."

Mark handed the preliminary forensics report to John. He noticed there wasn't a coffee cup in Mason's hand.

"No coffee yet?" Mark asked.

"Met a friend for coffee before I came in," John said as he sat. "Have Bookman's financials come in yet?"

"They should start trickling in this morning."

Mason thought for a minute. "He probably had a maid service. Check his address book."

Mark nodded. "I'll check." He jotted *Maid service?* on a notepad. "You called next of kin yesterday, right?"

It was Mason's turn to nod. "Yeah. They were *really* pleasant. 'So, our son's life finally caught up with him.' Anything from the M.E.?"

"The preliminary just said what you saw at the scene: Small caliber gunshot to the head." Mark handed John the summary

43

sheet. "No residue around the wound or on his clothing, so somebody shot him from several yards away. There's no obvious evidence the body was moved, but on a hard floor you might not see traces anyway."

"Didn't see an exit wound," Mason said, "so that's consistent. The bullet is probably still in his head. It won't tell us anything."

"How come?"

"The lack of powder and fingerprints tells me it was a pro. A .22 is inexpensive: One kill and it's at the bottom of the Hootch." Mason used a common nickname for the Chattahoochee River. He went on. "You said two things stood out. What besides the lack of material evidence?"

Mark thumbed pages. "The bit Officer Caligari turned up in canvassing about the woman seen leaving Bookman's house in the wee hours." Mark handed John the relevant page from the folder of canvass interviews.

"Was it recent?"

"Most recent was about a week ago," Mark said. "But if we can track her down, she might be able to give us background information. It's worth a shot anyhow."

"Check with vice," Mason said, "local and around the area, for call girls. If she's a pro, she might cooperate."

"Really?"

"Yeah. She might get someone to look away later if she cooperates in a murder investigation," John said. "Is the description good enough?"

"It's a good start. Average height, wears platform shoes and has really long hair. Might be a wig. But here's the thing that sets her apart: She drives herself. In a sedan. In the middle of the night. If she's a pro, she's either independent or works for someone who trusts her."

"And if she's just a friend?"

"Then she's probably in the address book."

Alcalá half shut his eyes.

After a moment, Mason said, "Gimme the inventory sheet."

"Stuff we took or furnishings?"

"Both."

The junior detective opened his eyes and found the correct folders, then handed John several stapled pages.

John looked through it all, then handed it back and asked, "What's missing?"

"Huh?"

"What should be here that isn't? You've got a guy who hasn't hit middle age, tech savvy, lives very comfortably. What isn't here?"

Mark scanned the pages. "Two nice TVs. The usual appliances. Wait ... where ... where's his phone? Everybody has a phone. He didn't have a land line, so he must have had a cell. And you said 'tech savvy,' so where's his computer? He should have at least one, maybe more. Was the phone in the garage or in one of his cars, maybe?"

"No, Welch's people would have found it."

Mark tapped on his desk. "Welch. That reminds me," he said. "She brought this envelope by around eight o'clock and told me to put it in your hands myself. I forgot it because she dropped it off just as I got here, and I put the other reports on top of it."

"Ah."

Alcalá handed Mason a nine-by-twelve manila envelope

marked *Detective Mason, Eyes Only*; papers inside were about a quarter inch thick.

"Did she say anything else?"

"No — look, there's a sticky on the back."

John flipped the envelope over and saw the yellow note. On it was the number twenty. He nodded and said, "You go ahead and start the calls to vice departments."

Mark nodded. "How far away do you want me to go?"

"Start with a ten-mile radius. Have you got a copy of the address book yet?"

"Yeah." Mark handed over a sheaf of paper. "I got Forensics to make two copies."

"Cool." Mason started leafing through his copy. "You get going on the calls."

Mark nodded, pulled out his list of area police departments dialed the first one.

John opened the envelope from Welch and pulled out a handwritten note. He read it and closed his eyes for a minute; Mark's voice fuzzed out on him. When he opened them a couple of minutes later, Mark was finishing up his first call.

"What'd you find out?"

"Alpharetta has two or three working girls who might fit the description. Do you want me to interview them?"

"Make all the calls first, then we'll talk to the most likely. I'm going to Bookman's house. I probably won't be back until after lunch."

"Okay, see you."

"Not so fast," Mason said. "If the FBI guys come by, make sure they get a copy of everything. Corral one of those summer interns to make copies."

Alcalá nodded.

Mason took a copy of Bookman's address book and the envelope Mark had handed him, and he left the squad room. But before going to the crime scene, he went by forensics.

"John," Welch said. "You're earlier than I expected."

"Met a friend early. Can you come with me to the Bookman house this morning?"

"How long do you think we'll be?"

"Could be there half an hour, could be the rest of the morning."

"Can you wait ten minutes, or do you want me to meet you there?"

"Meet me there. I'm going to drive through for a cup of coffee on the way. Can I get you one?"

"How 'bout a chai latte with one NutraSweet?"

"Foo-foo tea huh?" Mason grinned.

Maddie grinned. "If we're a long time, you'll have to buy me lunch, too. Do I need any special equipment?"

"Dunno. That's what we're going to find out."

"I'll drive a van."

10:32 a.m.

At Bookman's house, Mason spoke to the uniformed officers watching the house from a black-and-white out front. They drove off as Maddie Welch drove up in the forensics van.

"Letting them go, John?"

"They've been here since five. Had 'em doing walk-around three or four times every hour. Since we're here, I told 'em to go get something to eat and come back."

Welch nodded as she ducked under the crime scene tape

Mason held up for her. Mason, more than a foot taller, stepped over the tape.

While Mason fished for the door key in his pocket, Maddie asked, "I guess you went over the addendum."

"That's why we're here."

"And why did we keep this from the Bureau types?"

"Because it's our crime scene; because if there's something that I have to turn over to them, I will. But before I do, I want to know whether it's relevant to the case; and because they have not been forthcoming about why they're here."

As John opened the door, his cell phone beeped once, signaling an incoming text message. He looked at the message, then said, "Alcalá says the FBI agents are on their way here. We have about twenty minutes to find out what we can."

Maddie walked inside the house while John replied to the message. He followed her into the hallway.

"I should have suspected something was up in here," he said.

The hallway was around six feet by twelve, with a couple of chairs. It seemed to be a sort of sitting room or ante-room for the home office and the master suite. Two large, artsy photographs hung on the walls on opposite sides, both lit by track lighting.

"Which end?"

"This one," Welch said, standing by a Scottish landscape, framed to roughly twenty-four inches high by thirty-four wide. She pulled the right side of the picture frame. It rotated on the hinged left side, revealing a safe embedded in the wall. The safe looked to be fourteen inches wide by twelve tall; the nameplate that said *Swanson* flanked by two key locks.

"The inventory showed a keyring," John said. "Do any of the keys we found match this?"

"Oddly, two of them do. And they are very different keys."

"Did you open it?"

"No, we wouldn't do that without you here. But did you hear what I said ..."

"... about the keys? Yes, I got it. If it's sophisticated enough, the wrong key could destroy the contents. Or one could be the key to a matching safe somewhere else, maybe even here in the house."

"Not in the house," Maddie said. "You wanted every square foot sounded, and you got it. This is the only one."

John nodded.

Maddie asked, "How about a double-door safe? You know, a safe within a safe."

"Not likely with both keys on the same ring. And the wall's not that thick behind it."

"Do we have time to work out which key to try?"

"No," Mason said. "And we aren't going to. I'm going to find out what safe company installed it. If they have keys and they're bonded, I'll have them open it."

When the FBI agents, Orozco and Grove, arrived a few minutes later, Mason and Welch were talking about the lack of gunshot residue and any electronics in the house. They were *not* talking about the wall safe.

The four of them discussed the overview of the forensics from the preliminary report, and all agreed the electronics were probably stolen.

"After all," Mason said, "if the gear was high-end enough, taking it might have been sufficient to form a motive. In that case, Bookman surprised the thief and was shot."

Orozco nodded noncommittally; Grove didn't indicate agreement or disagreement.

1:34 p.m.

Mason followed Lieutenant Tejeda into Captain Berman's office. Even though there were chairs for them, space was tight because the desk was more than halfway through the room due to Berman's immense girth.

"Yes, sir?" Tejeda said.

Berman said, "I'm getting pressure from Rusher to explain what's going on with the Bookman investigation."

Brian Rusher was one of two majors in the department.

"Meaning . . . ?" Mason asked.

"He says he's getting requests from the FBI to turn everything over to them." He looked at Tejeda. "Sergio, is there any reason we should hold on to this?"

Tejeda, who was four inches taller than Mason, shifted, trying to find a comfortable place for his knees.

"There's no indication of a Federal crime, Captain. Nothing, absolutely nothing, links this to anything the Bureau has a mandate to investigate. Unless you or Major Rusher or somebody has information that we don't, I say they're trying to mark off some new territory."

"Mason," the captain said, "you knew Nathan Bookman."

Mason nodded.

"Is there any reason to suspect he might have been involved in a federal crime?"

"The only thing I can think of is the one sighting we had last Fall in connection with the Jamison case." Mason didn't mention his speculation about Kaiser Transceivers.

"The little red sports car?"

Mason nodded. "It was in his garage."

"Yeah," Berman said, "I can see that having white-collar crime implications. Are you keeping anything back that might indicate that's what Bookman was into?"

Tejeda, who knew about the extra work the forensics team had done, since he had to approve their overtime, glanced at Mason.

Mason said, "No. And they will be getting everything we have."

Tejeda motioned with one hand and said, "The evidence we have to date shows no indication of going that direction."

"Well, then ... ideas?"

"How about this?" Tejeda said. "How about we make them part of the investigation? As soon as something says federal crime, we give it to them."

Mason and the captain both nodded.

"I can sell that," the captain said. "We give them actual work on the case, even get some budget relief, but keep it local until something bigger shows up."

"Is there ... ?" Mason paused. "Can we find out what these guys want?"

No one said anything.

"Wait!" Mason said. "I know a couple of Federal prosecutors. How about I give them a call and see what they can tell me?"

Berman threw an open hand and nodded. Mason and Tejeda left his office.

Tejeda drew himself up to his full six feet, five inches, and asked Mason, "How do you know these prosecutors?"

"They're prosecuting the fallout from Jamison's death last fall."

"Okay. Do you want me to talk with Grove and Orozco?

Where do you want them to start?"

"Go see Mark and get the names of the people from Bookman's address book. Most were sports car enthusiasts, meaning they have at least some money — there's the white collar angle again — and some will be more willing to talk to the Bureau than with us anyhow."

Mason stopped in front of the break room while Tejeda nodded and went into the restroom.

Mason got his coffee mug. At the coffee pot, he sniffed, frowned, poured out the dregs and started a new pot.

As he leaned against the counter awaiting the black gold, he saw Mark pass by in the hallway.

"Mark!"

Mark stopped. "Hey."

"Are you headed to your desk?"

"Yeah, why?"

"Tejeda's coming by. Give him a copy of Bookman's address book."

"No problem, but what's it for?"

"Our fibbie friends are going do some of the interviews."

"I'll get started right away. Tell me more later."

When the coffee was ready, Mason poured his mug and went outside to the picnic tables. He put in a call to the US Attorney's office and asked to speak to Ms DeRaveniere.

"I'm afraid she is not in the office, Detective," the receptionist said. "Would you like to leave a voice mail?"

"Okay. Wait ... Is Boris Stolzfus in?"

"Yes, sir. Hold on a minute."

Half a minute later, Stolzfus came on the line. They exchanged greetings and one-sentence catch-ups.

"I'd bring Emily in, but she's in court this morning with

some motions in a prosecution you're familiar with. Were you calling about that?"

"Like the string that walked back into the bar, I'm afraid not."

Stolzfus snorted. "So, what can I do for you?"

"This is a Justice Department question. I have a couple of FBI agents trying to participate in a local murder case, but they're being very hush-hush about why they want in. I was wondering if you could find out anything for me."

"I'll see what I can do. Let me grab a pen ... Okay what are the names?"

"Robert Grove and Victor Orozco." Mason read the agent's badge numbers from the crime scene log to Stolzfus. "Whatever you're allowed to tell me will be fine."

"Okay, I'll see what I can find out."

After they rang off, Mason went back to his desk.

"I have the list ready for the Loo," Mark said.

"Thanks."

Mason turned to reports that had come in since the morning.

Still no real evidence.

Mason drummed his fingers and started to get up. His cell phone rang, and he sat back down.

"Mason."

"John, it's Boris."

"What can you tell me?"

"I can't tell you."

"Huh?"

"But if you follow along, I'll tell you what I *can* tell you, and whatever remains ... You know the rest."

"Got it."

"Look up a list of Bureau directorates. Read them off to me."

One by one Mason read off the list of major divisions.

Stolzfus was responding: "Nope ... No ... Not them ... No ... No ... skip to the next one; yes, I mean that."

"Thanks, Boris."

"Glad to be unhelpful."

They rang off.

Mason sat and thought for a few minutes.

When Lieutenant Tejeda approached Mark's desk. Mark handed him the list.

Mason waved to the two of them to follow him. They squeezed into Captain Berman's office and closed the door.

"Why are you all here?"

"Because," Mason said, "the FBI agents, Grove and Orozco: They aren't from the Bureau's white-collar crime division."

"So, where?"

"They're from counter-intelligence."

1:57 p.m.

Back at their desks, Mason asked Alcalá about his progress in calling area police departments.

"I've talked to all the vice units in the radius, except Atlanta, which is right on the edge."

"And?"

"We have six likely and four more possibles."

Mason said, "You kept a copy of Bookman's address book, right?"

"Yeah."

"Any of these women appear in there?"

"Haven't checked yet."

"While you're checking, I'm going to pick up some lunch to bring back. Can I get you something?"

"Five Guys, maybe?"

"Sounds good. Split an order of fries?"

Mark assented and gave John his burger order and cash to cover his part.

John drove to pick up the food.

When he returned, John put Mark's bag on the corner of his desk and said, "Your receipt and change are in the bag. What have you got on phone numbers?"

"Thanks for picking this up. None of the contact numbers I got from the departments was in the address book. I even checked for swapped digits, backward numbers, that kind of thing."

"Hmm," John said through a mouthful of burger, nodding. He chewed and swallowed and said, "Thorough. Good. Show me your list."

Mark passed John the list and took a sip from his drink, then swallowed and said, "Looks like three to the west and three to the south."

"Okay. I'll take west, you take south. Since you were looking through the address book anyway, did you see anything interesting?"

"A handful of female names. A collection of numbers listed under a car club. Oh, and I got the number for Bookman's house cleaning service. I'm going to call them after I eat."

"Okay. They won't know anything, but call them anyway." Mason put a couple of fries in his mouth. After he swallowed, he said, "Tell you what: Hand off the working girls to a couple of plain-clothes officers. You and I will split the women who *are* in the book. We'll give the car club to the Bureau guys."

Mark nodded as he chewed.

While they were eating, an intern brought in the copy of the case file they had ordered for the FBI agents.

Mason nodded thanks to the intern, who retreated to another room. "How many addresses are in Bookman's address book? For women, I mean."

"Ones that aren't named Bookman? Four."

"How many do we have addresses for?"

"Only one."

"Okay, you take that one. I'll call the others to set up appointments."

"Okay," Mark said, standing. "Can I get your trash?"

"No, thanks; not done yet."

When Mark got back from throwing away his trash and washing his hands, John asked, "What're the last names on my three calls?"

"Langley, Smith, and Franzetti."

"What, no Frohike or Byers?"

Mark's eyes narrowed, then he snickered. "After all," he said, "there was only *one* gunman."

John smiled and picked up his last French fry.

Mark said, "I'll go find a couple of guys to work the prostitute angle."

While John was chewing the last bite, he gathered his trash and took it to the large, lidded trash bin labeled "Time Sensitive Waste." After he washed up and returned to his desk, he started on the phone numbers of the women Alcalá had named.

He first checked and found that two of the numbers, Patricia Smith and Cynthia Langley, were for cell phones; Lucia

Franzetti's number was a land line.

He only spoke with one, Cynthia Langley ("call me Cindy"), and made an appointment to meet her at her office. He left messages for the other two: Franzetti's on an answering machine, Smith's on voice mail provided by the phone company.

While John was leaving a voice mail for Ms Smith, Mark came back and called Ruth Sellers, the remaining female name in Nathan Bookman's address book. She answered right away, and he made an appointment to meet her.

2:58 p.m.

Mason arrived at Cindy Langley's office late — late for him anyway: he habitually arrived for appointments five minutes early.

He took the two remaining minutes to review the background material he had found about Ms Langley: age twenty-eight, never married, ran a home decorating business out of a storefront in a strip shopping center a couple of blocks from the mall (consultations after eleven a.m. Wednesday through Sunday, and by appointment any other time), drove an Avalon.

Inside, he found the office decorated in wood and Italian leather, and a tall, broad-shouldered woman with bobbed blond hair that fell just below her jawline. She wore a white silk blouse with rounded collar points; tapered, black silk pants; and emerald jewelry. Mason thought, *If those stones are real, she's a lot more successful than even the decor indicates.*

He also realized she couldn't be the woman Nathan Bookman's neighbor described: she was at least five-feet-ten in low-heeled shoes.

"Detective Mason?" she asked.

"That's me. Ms Langley?"

She nodded and held out a hand and said, "I'm pleased to meet you. What can I do for you?"

"Do you know Nathan Bookman?"

Cindy smiled and said, "Yes, Book and I go back a few years. Last fall, I did the interior design when he remodeled his house. Is he in some kind of trouble?"

"I'm afraid he's dead."

Those words damped all motion, damped all sound, damped time itself.

As Ms Langley gradually returned to normal speed, she exhaled and said, "I'm very sorry to hear that. As I said, he was a friend as well as a client. How did he die?"

"He was murdered."

Her eyes opened big and round, and she looked at the carpet for a moment.

"Had you seen him recently?"

"No, we haven't — hadn't — seen each other for several weeks. Why did you contact me, Detective?"

"Your name and number were in Mr Bookman's personal address book. I hate to push into your personal space, but it's my job to ask how well you knew him." Mason made it sound almost like a question.

"Well, we were friends for a year or so before he became my client. We meet — met — a couple of times a month. Usually at Santini's on 128 next to the coffee shop.

"We were ... involved ... after my work for him was finished, around January this year."

"And since then, your relationship ... cooled?"

She nodded in the affirmative.

"Again, I hate to pry, but because I need the most up-to-date information possible, I have to ask: Why did you stop seeing him romantically?"

"Because he started seeing ... professional women. If you get my drift. Frankly, I didn't want to risk the chance of disease."

"Can you help me place, in calendar time, when that happened?"

"Okay ... We met in August or September two years ago. We'd see each other once in a while when we were both out for drinks with friends. After a few weeks we exchanged phone numbers, then we went out one-on-one to dinner, movies and the like for a few weeks. We still saw our friends — I mean we didn't wall ourselves off or anything.

"When he bought his current house, early last year, he told me he didn't like the interior. It was dated, and it needed to be refreshed. He got various bids, including mine, and contracted my firm to do the work starting in September. In addition to design, we work as a general contractor, hiring subcontractors.

"We finished at the end of last year, right before Christmas. We became lovers after New Years."

"His house certainly seemed to be first class," Mason said. "It was very modern, but not cold."

"Thanks," Cindy said, smiling. "Anyway, we got closer in the winter — it was during the NFL playoffs. He was a fiend for sports statistics, and something about that and his generally ... I don't know ... breezy? ... that'll do ... his breezy attitude combined with great intelligence intrigued me. But I was driven away when I found out about the prostitutes."

"When was that?"

"This past April. Book didn't complain when I fenced myself off. He even offered to pay my doctor bills if I had caught anything from him."

"How did you find out about the prostitutes?"

"One night we were having drinks at Santini's. We were planning on one drink and going to my place, but he met this guy he knew. Anyhow, they huddled together like thieves for almost an hour, and I started talking to a girl, a little brunette who was hanging around like she wanted to meet the other guy, and when Book and I finally left we went to his house because it was half as far away and it was late. There was a car in the driveway with a woman in the driver's seat, and it was obvious what was going on."

"Did *he* say she was a prostitute? Did you see money or anything else change hands?"

"No. But regular women don't dress like that. *Party girls* don't dress like that."

"Can you describe her?"

"About my height but wearing platforms so maybe five-five or five-six; long hair, like midway down her back; barely wore a tube top and a very short, tight skirt or maybe short shorts; deeply tanned, but no tan lines. The few words I heard her speak sounded like a strong Southern or Western accent."

Mason nodded. "That's consistent with a description we got from another source."

"So, you know who she is." Ms Langley's eyes narrowed a little as she watched for Mason's reaction.

Mason showed a little smile. "Not yet."

Cindy gave a little *of course* nod.

"Did your business relationship end when you broke up?"

"No. That was completed before we started 'contact sports'."

"About refurbishing his house, what can you tell me about his wall safe?"

"When he made that a line item in the contract, I told him I don't usually do security, but I could recommend someone. He said thanks, but he wanted me to contract it even if it cost more, which of course it did. Most clients who want a safe will contract for the work directly with the security company."

Mason pressed his lips together as he chose his next question.

"Were any special measures taken when the safe was installed? I mean, was the safe an off-the-shelf model he simply had installed in the wall or were any special measures taken to ensure the security of the safe itself?"

"Just a moment." Cindy turned to her computer, clicked, and typed for a moment. "It was an off-the-shelf Swanson double-key-lock safe, model twenty-five dash six twenty-four. It was installed by Ribo Security."

Mason knew who he would be calling on next. And he wouldn't be waiting for the break of day.

3:05 p.m.

Ruth Sellers opened her front door for Mark Alcalá. She wore a low-cut, black camisole and dark jeans over her thin, top-heavy figure; white athletic socks covered her feet. Thick, mahogany hair fell down her back, just a couple of inches short of her waist; the occasional curl added interest. In her small, round face, she had amplified her already large eyes with makeup, so she almost resembled a Japanese cartoon; the rest of the makeup was very light over her deep tan.

She showed Mark to the sofa in the middle of her studio apartment, and when she asked, "Can you wait here just a minute?" she sounded like all the drawls in West Texas had been distilled into a single shot glass, and she had just downed it.

He nodded and she walked behind him; he heard her open the wardrobe door and close it; when she came back a moment later, her arms were in an unbuttoned, short-sleeved, plaid shirt, and she carried cowboy boots.

"I hope you don't mind, but I only have about fifteen minutes before I have to leave for work." She set the boots down and began to button the shirt. "And please call me Ruthie."

"Where do you work?" Mark asked.

"At Chaps & Spurs in Buckhead. It's a Western bar." She stopped buttoning halfway up; the edges of her cami just showed. "Today I'm covering happy hour and the first part of the evening. I'll get off around ten and be home by ten forty-five. Now, what did you want to see me about, Detective?" When she bent over and pulled up her jeans to put on a boot, Mark could see her socks were calf-length.

Before he could reply, she said, " 'Alcalá' sounds Spanish, but you don't look it. Where are you from?"

"I grew up on a farm outside Minneapolis. My great grand-father escaped Spain just before the start of World War Two and moved to the Upper Midwest. I'm descended from one Spaniard and a flock of Norwegians. Weirdly, for Americans, they kept the accent over that final a."

"So why are you here to see me?"

He said, "This is a little awkward. I came to tell you that someone you know has died."

Ruthie pushed down the jeans leg over her first boot. Her

eyebrows dropped, pushing the corners of her mouth into a frown.

"Who was it?" She looked into his eyes.

"Nathan Bookman."

Her eyes widened, then rounded, then welled up and shone. A tear or two wandered down her face. "Nathan. Bookman."

Mark nodded.

Her eyes closed, expelling more tears.

"Was he in a wreck in one of his stupid-fast cars?"

"No. I'm ... afraid he was shot."

"In a bar someplace?"

"His body was found in his living room."

"And why did you come to tell *me*?"

Mark said, "Because your name was in his address book. We're contacting people he knew in the hope that we can learn something that might help us find out who did this."

"What can I help you with?" She opened her eyes, now red.

Mark's eyes were stuck to hers. "What can you tell us about his friends, his house? Did he have any jewelry or other valuables? Did you ever go out together? And I have to ask how close you were."

"If he had any valuables, he kept them in the safe behind that picture in the hall. I mean, his house was nice and all, but he didn't have any really valuable art — except maybe a painting, but why didn't he have that in the living room? — didn't have any jewelry to speak of, didn't have anything really expensive except the cars. Were *they* all right?"

Mark nodded. "Yes. Both cars were intact in his garage. Did he like to talk about them?"

A little smile traced her lips. "He loved the little red one. I think he got the big gray one to impress other guys. It *was* more comfortable to ride in."

"So, you rode in his cars?"

"Yeah. I'd go to his house after work, and we'd go for a drive, especially on summer nights, while it was still warm but before the humidity went back up. Moonlit drives around Lake Lanier can be pretty nice. Then we'd go back to his place."

"Did you stay the rest of the night?"

"Not usually. We'd have a drink and a tumble in the sheets, then make omelets or pancakes or something and I'd go back home."

"How often?"

"Most weeks."

"You went to his house after work. Out for a drive in good weather, back to his place. Did anyone ever see you together?"

She shook her head. "Strictly under cover. So to speak." She snickered at her unintended double meaning. "He said something about a client who wanted him on the straight and narrow, but I never found out who it was."

"On all these drives you never stopped anywhere? Other than traffic signals, I mean? Not a diner or a Waffle House or anything?"

"No," she said. "Well, we went to Waffle House one time. But just once."

"When you were at his house, did you ever meet anyone coming or going?"

"One night a couple of months ago, he wasn't home when I got there, so I waited in my car. He drove up and parked in the garage, but some woman parked behind my car and when she saw me, she went ballistic and got louder and louder until she told him they were through. What, did she think she was his only woman or something? I didn't have *that* illusion."

She paused a moment, then her eyes cleared, and her face straightened out.

"Thanks for coming by. I'm really sorry about Book, but I really don't think I know anything that could help your investigation."

She glanced at the door.

"I hope you don't mind," she said, "but I really need to leave for work now."

"No problem," Mark said, handing her a business card. "I'll let myself out."

As he was closing the front door, he glanced back through and saw Ruthie's face twist in anguish; the closing door cut short the sound of her sob.

4:00 p.m.

Ruthie barely made the drive to work at Chaps & Spurs. She drove robotically, not noticing the traffic around her, stopping, slowing, turning without thinking. She knew her evening would be spent longing for the drinks she would be serving to others. Maybe some nice pseudo-cowboy would buy her a drink. Or maybe Gerald, the bartender.

At least now she knew why Book hadn't come to the bar Wednesday night. It wasn't because he was seeing someone else.

Maybe someone would offer to take her home and she'd have a shot at forgetting for an evening.

Gerald wouldn't, of course. His boyfriend would object.

When Ruthie started at C&S, she had offered him all her charms. She quit trying after Gerald whispered to her that he was gay. She kept his secret — a western bar in Atlanta with a straight clientele was not the place to out yourself. Besides, Gerald steered business toward Ruthie when she was working, and he had helped her find a cheap apartment in the suburbs. She suspected he did it to help her stay out of trouble. Gerald was a friend.

Maybe someone *would* offer to take her home. But it wouldn't be the same. Not the same as Book.

Maybe she wouldn't want someone for the night after all. Better to hurt alone and be done with it than paint over the pain with pretended affection.

Business started slow that night. Ruthie unconsciously went from customer to customer, caring for the minutiae without really paying attention. Greeting, taking orders, serving, following up, cleaning up, even the light-hearted flirting that made her one of the bar's best waitresses. Every move, every giggle, every wink, every wiggle was on autopilot.

As the evening wore on and business picked up, Ruthie wore down.

Eventually, she asked Gerald to ask the manager to call someone to work the rest of her shift. A few minutes later, Gerald motioned her over and told her that Janae would be in to cover for her in fifteen minutes.

"What's the matter?" he asked.

"I got some bad news," she said. Talking to him, her face relaxed from forced pert and sassy to fatigued and weary. "I don't think I'll be able to sleep tonight. How much is a bottle of VO?"

He told her, and she fished the cash out of her tips. He

wrapped the bottle in a paper bag.

When she had finished up and handed off her tables to her replacement, she took the bottle and drove home.

8:30 p.m.

At home, Ruthie put a couple of ice cubes in a tumbler, filled it with whiskey, and then left it to sit and cool and let the pungent aroma pervade the room while she shucked her boots and jeans and shirt and pulled on pajama pants with her camisole. Sitting at one end of the couch, the end with a small table and lamp and a coaster, she took a long breath over her drink and began to remember.

She remembered her dad yelling at her mother and calling her names a ten-year-old didn't understand. She remembered her mother being cowed and submissive and afraid. She remembered that lasting for years and years. She remembered coming home from school when she was fourteen and seeing police cars in front of her house. And glancing back from her aunt's car, and a policewoman leading her mother, who wore handcuffs. And the trial and the jury finding her mother not guilty and her mother coming home and Dad's recliner was gone. And remembering the names her dad had used and learning what they meant and her mother deserving them now if not before.

Ruthie took a sip of her whiskey.

She remembered high school and boys and her mother saying boys always lie and learning it was true the hard way. And when she was eighteen leaving Odessa and driving to Plano and getting a job as a waitress in a diner. From there to Bossier

City and then Jackson, more waitressing, and repeating it all in Birmingham.

By the time she arrived in Atlanta, she had a beat-up car and a twenty-first birthday and knew how to dress western on a budget. The job at Chaps & Spurs was easy to get because she looked and sounded the part.

And she had met Nathan Bookman — Book.

She pulled a long, slow tug on her drink and swallowed it a little bit at a time.

One night a couple of years ago, Book wandered in, dressed the part of someone who went to urban western bars: a black silk shirt, cut western but untrimmed; jeans faded with wear; cowboy boots a color somewhere between brown and cordovan, with steel toes. Ruthie served him his drink, and they joked back and forth. He came back a couple of times a week, and he began to wait for one of her tables when her section was crowded. Eventually, he took her home. And they continued meeting, even after she realized he wasn't reserving himself for her exclusively, because when they were together, at least for a few hours, there wasn't anyone else.

Ruthie took one more sip from her drink and then set the glass on the coaster. She felt the dullness of the alcohol creeping over her. Why bother folding out the bed?

She remembered Book taking her for rides in his fancy cars and treating her like a lady. And unlike the college students back home, he never lied to her. The only time he didn't tell her something she asked was one of their rides by the river. She was *so* drunk that night. They made a stop, and he wouldn't tell her why. Not that she cared by that point.

But the cute policeman ... Would he want to know about that?

The whiskey won: Ruthie closed her eyes and forgot.

Saturday, June 23

10:00 a.m.

Mark Alcalá looked unhappy, verging on angry.

Mark asked, "Did you know Bookman had a safe in the wall?"

"Yeah," Mason said sheepishly. "'Fraid so. Learned about it in the preliminary supplemental report from forensics."

"Prelim ..." Mark looked at the tip of his nose. "Oh. You mean the envelope Welch left for you yesterday." He glanced back at John. "Is there a reason you kept this from me?"

"It's because the Bureau guys were looking for it. Remember all that foot-tapping Grove was doing? They were looking for something in particular, and I thought it might be a floor safe. I wanted the heads-up on it. Had to pay forensics twenty hours overtime to look for that and anything else structural that the feds might be interested in. And *you* weren't told about it in case you were asked."

Mark whistled. "You wanted that pretty bad. Why does it matter?"

"Ironically, Maddie's people would have found it anyway, without looking hard. I wanted to know first because if the Bureau gets hold of the evidence, it'll be harder to get it back. This is a local case so far, and if we can keep it that way, we should. What did you find out from Ruth Sellers?"

"She and Bookman were having late-night rendezvous, she almost never stayed the whole night. She usually left before dawn."

"Was she the woman the neighbor saw?"

"She matches the description, and the way they were meeting fits with the times around one a.m., so yeah, it was her. How about you with Langley?"

"Cindy Langley was another of Bookman's amorous adventures, but when she found out about Sellers, she broke up with him."

"Jealous type."

"Maybe, or she just didn't like being deceived. Did Ruth mention any other women?"

"She said she met someone one night; it might have been Langley. But Ruthie knew she wasn't Bookman's one and only."

" 'Ruthie'?"

"She said to call her that."

Mason scrunched his mouth up for a second. "How did you find out about the safe?"

"Didn't I say? Ruthie mentioned knowing about the safe in the wall behind the picture."

Mason's phone rang; it was the duty sergeant. "Detective Mason, there's some people here to see you. Gave the name of Bookman."

Mason nodded and said, "Thanks." To Alcalá he said,

72

"There went my afternoon interview."

He looked around the room, and called out to Officer Caligari, who was just coming in.

"Caligari, are you busy for ten or fifteen minutes?"

Caligari stopped and looked around to find the source.

"No, Detective, what can I do for you?"

"I need you to go to the lobby and retrieve a couple of visitors: Mr and Mrs Bookman. Bring them to the conference room. The door will be open, and you'll see Mark and me in there."

Caligari's eyes widened when she recognized the name. She nodded and spun on the balls of her feet to head up front.

To Alcalá, Mason said, "Come meet Bookman's parents with me."

At the entrance to the small conference room, Mason flipped the sign on the door, and he and Alcalá went in to stand and wait.

Mark asked, "What were you doing this afternoon?"

"I was going to talk to the people who installed the safe to make sure there aren't any surprises when we open it."

Caligari returned with an older couple in tow.

Both appeared to be in their mid-sixties, the man was about five feet, six inches; the woman, the same height in heels, but her gray beehive added about four more inches; her makeup was sparse, the colors chosen badly and emphasized rather than concealed the frown permanently etched into her face; the skirt of her dark suit fell well below her knee. The man's black suit was clean; his shirt, white and starched; his tie, electric blue; his shoes, well-polished black wingtips; his dark gray hair was slick and not moving, which just as well because he had combed about a third of what he needed over his pattern baldness, drawing attention rather than disguising; the combover was perched atop a grimace of eternal disgust.

Caligari said, "Detective Mason, this is Mr and Mrs Bookman."

Mason extended a hand to introduce himself and offer condolences, then introduced the Bookmans to Alcalá. They all sat down. Alcalá asked whether they wanted coffee, which they politely refused.

James Bookman asked, "What can you tell us about our son's death?" His tinny voice was pitched rather high, and to Mason's ear, annoying.

Mason deferred to Caligari, who told about the discovery of their son's body, leading up to the detectives being called to the scene. After James asked her a couple of questions about minor details, Mason let Caligari escape.

Mason described the scene in a general way, and asked, "What can you tell us about your son?"

James said, "Nathan was always a wayward son, doing things we had forbidden, even thinking up naughty things to do we hadn't thought of. He was always involved with some girl —"

"At *least* it was a girl!" Joyce cut in, her voice nasal, unpleasant, deep — deeper than her husband's — and rasped like a thirty-year chain-smoker.

"Yes, Mother, they were girls. And he drank. As far as I know he never used any drugs."

Mason asked, "When was the last time you saw him?"

"It was at Christmas."

"Six months ago," Alcalá said.

Joyce said, "It was the day *after* Christmas. Our son couldn't be bothered to come home for the holiday itself."

Mason glanced at Joyce's hands: no nicotine stains. "Why was that?" he asked.

"He said it was connected with his work, whatever that was — he never would tell us. But in reality, it was after he asked if he could bring a girl down, and we said, no, it was just going to be the four of us."

"Did Nathan have a brother or a sister?"

"Neither," Joyce said. "My mother was going to be there, and she would not have sat at the dinner table with someone we assumed Nathan was regularly doing you-know-what with."

"That was *her* attitude. What was yours?"

"As long as they acted civilly and slept separately, we would allow her to come."

James said, "But Nathan wouldn't have brought her anyway."

"Why was that?"

"Because we were obligated tell them their behavior was going to send them to Hell."

"And Nathan wouldn't take kindly to that?"

"It was worse, much worse," Joyce said. "He would *laugh* at it. There was no end to my son's disrespect of his own parents. In Old Testament times he would have been stoned."

James added, "And then they would talk about the bars and the parties and the lascivious movies they went to all the time."

Joyce continued, "And he spoke of a huge television in his bedroom. He probably watched filth in there before doing filth himself."

This had gone on long enough, so Mason decided to see whether there was anything they could add to his murder investigation. "I appreciate your candor in telling us about your son's background," he said. "Do you know of anyone who might have reason to harm him, to kill him?"

"You need to understand," Joyce said, "we saw our son once or twice a year. We didn't know any associates or coworkers."

James added, "If you want my advice, you should check the loose women he saw. See whether one of *them* had a husband or boyfriend."

Mason nodded; Alcalá made a note in his notepad.

"Is there a chance," James asked, "that we could see our son's house today?"

Mason nodded. "That won't be a problem. Mark, can you come with us?"

Alcalá assented, and as they left the conference room Mason flipped the sign back to "AVAILABLE".

The Bookmans followed Mason and Alcalá to the crime scene.

During the drive Mark asked, "Why did you ask if I could come?"

"It's part of the show for the victim's family. For the investigation, there are two of them, so if they split up going around the house, we'll make sure neither one is left alone. For them, they need to know that you have a responsible position."

11:04 a.m.

At the house, just inside the front door, Mason said, "This is where Nathan's body was found."

Joyce Bookman's face screwed up tight. "Did Nathan keep the house so badly that it smelled like this?"

Alcalá said, "I'm afraid that the body — your son's body, I

mean — well, with the body relaxing at death, all the, um, material that's normally held in check until we find it convenient to dispose of it was expelled."

After a moment to consider this and understand it, James asked, "Was there much blood?"

"No, sir. There was a single, small-caliber gunshot to his head. There was just a trickle of blood that didn't drop to the floor."

Joyce asked, "Did he suffer?"

"No. His death would have been instant."

Her countenance soured.

Mason hadn't thought it possible for her to look more unapproving.

She said, "I'm certain he's suffering now."

She closed her eyes and shook her head. "Would it be all right if I look around?"

"Yes, ma'am," Mason said. "Mark, would you show Mrs Bookman around?"

Alcalá nodded, and as they walked away, he asked, "Are you familiar with the house?"

As they disappeared through the door to the kitchen, Mason turned to James. "Do you know your son had a safe in the house?"

James blinked three or four times. "He may have mentioned he was having a safe installed when he was redecorating last year, but it was just in passing."

After a brief pause, James put in, "Detective, we didn't approve of the way Nathan lived, but we approve even less of murder. Do everything you can to find his killer."

"Mr Bookman, I bet there are a lot of things we disagree

about, but this is not one of them."

2:00 p.m.

Clarissa Miller was all smiles and humming something familiar as she entered the Penfields' kitchen.

Gloria Heinmeier, Ron Penfield's mother-in-law, poured boiling water from the kettle into the teapot. "You seem to be feeling better," she said.

"*Much* better," Clarissa said. "The pain from the other day is all gone, and I got ... something in the mail."

Gloria waited, and when Clarissa continued to smile and hum, and added pacing and circulating hands to the mix, but saying nothing else, Gloria said, "Out with it! What has you in such a good mood?"

Clarissa stopped short and made *I'm telling you* motions with her hands, but she said nothing — her smile prevented words from making their way out.

Suddenly, she laughed, long and hard, and when her breath had given out and she had inhaled deeply, she (finally!) said, "When Abe —" at that she nearly choked as laughter exploded up from her toes, and she twittered as her air expired again.

She held her lips between her teeth to try to regain composure. After ten or fifteen seconds, she again attempted coherence.

"When Abe and I were married, we bought life insurance. I figured that when he left me, he'd reassign his beneficiary to his new wife. I reassigned mine, mostly to my mother." Her face scrunched momentarily. "But he apparently got never got around to changing his policy to benefit Sharon, not even over ten months of living together and eight more of marriage."

Gloria checked the tea in the pot and decided it needed to steep another minute. "It's none of my business," she said, "but you seem to be saying it's a pretty sum."

"It's enough to pay off my mortgage *and* my credit cards," Clarissa said. "*And* I'll be able to set some aside for emergencies."

Gloria was pouring out as she asked, "Did he leave nothing to his new wife?"

"I don't know," Clarissa said. "And I suppose I should care, but I don't right now." Her tone grew louder and more strident as she said, "That, I think, is part of the price she should pay for *stealing* my *husband*," till at the end she was almost shouting.

Gloria was stirring sugar into her cup, and she had set the honey next to Clarissa for hers.

"So now," Gloria asked, "how do you think your life will change — day to day, I mean?"

Clarissa's spoon clinked against the inside of her cup as she stirred. Her head tilted to one side, and she blinked several times as she thought. When she spoke, her naturally raspy voice spoke in a gravelly stage whisper. "I ... haven't thought about that. I suppose ... I guess ... maybe I could join a gym and get rid of some of this weight. After our divorce, I put it on to spite Abe. After that, overeating became a ... habit. Too much comfort from food? Too many hours filled with ... nothing to do and eating just to be occupied."

Clarissa paused and finally took a sip of her tea.

"I'm sorry to make you so serious," Gloria said. "Right now, enjoy the feeling and make firmer plans tomorrow."

Clarissa smiled a different smile, one of gratitude. "Tomorrow. Planning starts tomorrow."

Sunday, June 24

11:00 a.m.

Mason and Alcalá continued assembling the pieces of Nathan Bookman's life.

The sum of the interviews showed what Mason expected: Nathan Bookman had been a gregarious individual who routinely hid his genius; he drank, but not often to excess; he had some skill at wooing women across the short term; his business was "consulting," though the subject of his consultation was amorphous and no one could identify his clients or even what he consulted on.

The coroner's office called to ask Mason whether he wanted them to hold on to the remains.

Mason asked about the status, and when he heard that the samples had already been sent off for the second wave of toxicology reports, he told them to release the body to Nathan Bookman's parents.

When he rang off, Alcalá asked, "Why not hold the body, it might give us some leverage."

"Leverage over who? Or is it *whom*?"

"Bookman's parents?"

"Granted they're cretins, but the local police in Headland confirmed they were both at work on Wednesday and Thursday. No opportunity. Besides, can you see either of them pulling off something this cleanly?"

Alcalá rolled his eyes. "Yeah, you're right. Looks like we have to wait for something else to break. Where are we looking next?"

"Other than routine, the next thing we have is the funeral — the reason we release the body. We see who shows up, observe behavior."

"Okay. What's the plan?"

"It'll depend on whether James and Joyce have the service here or take him back to Alabama."

"If it's here?"

Mason drummed his fingers. "I'll be inside. You'll be outside photographing people and cars. We'll see about getting video inside."

"And if it's in Alabama?"

"I'll drive down and attend. I get to go because Book and I were acquainted."

"And I get the routine paperwork?"

"Yep."

"Great." Alcalá grimaced and shook his head slowly.

"Look, Mark, I don't do this lightly. You've got a good eye, better attention to detail than I've ever seen. Think of it as a visualization thing. See the puzzle come together. See where the gaps are for yourself. When I get back — or before I go if the funeral isn't for several days — give me a list of gaps in our knowledge."

A couple of hours later the assistant coroner called Mason to tell him that James and Joyce were having their son's body picked up by a local funeral home, and they had purchased a plot at the attached cemetery. Mason started the paperwork to requisition the people and equipment he would need for the surveillance he planned.

Just as he was getting started, Grove and Orozco, the FBI agents, walked into the squad room and up to Mason's desk.

John smiled and said, "Hey. What can I do for you?"

Orozco frowned.

Grove said, "We want to take the Bookman case off your hands."

John blinked a couple of times. "This seems," he said, drawing *seems* out, "like a perfectly simple local homicide. Why do you want to assert Federal jurisdiction here?"

"There are two reasons," Grove said. "First, as we told you before, Nathan Bookman was a person of interest in an ongoing investigation."

Mark asked, "What kind of investigation?"

"We can't share that with you," Orozco answered. "We can't afford for any details of our inquiries to get out. If we take the case, we can keep control of all the data, and your department has one case taken off its plate."

"All the data and all the evidence," John said. "What's the other reason?"

"Because you held back information about Bookman's safe." Grove said.

Orozco added, "We don't think we can trust you to share your information in real time."

Mason put on a Yoda voice. "Mm. Brass tacks, they came to."

Alcalá snorted lightly; Orozco chuckled once; Grove remained stone-faced.

Reverting to his normal voice, John said, "You will be there when we open the safe the first time. You have copies of all our documentation. Why do you think we were hiding something?"

"Because we caught the shenanigans with the report addendum. Why did you do the extra search, anyway?"

Mark raised his eyebrows and John nodded.

"Because," Mark said, "Bookman was peripherally implicated in the case of Senator Jamison's death last year."

John added, "We cooperated with the Federal prosecutors, and we wanted to know whether there was anything for them. Up to that point, there was never any documentation linking him to either the senator or the senator's death." He paused for a second. "And because I knew you were looking for the safe."

Mark tapped his foot three times, to Grove's annoyance.

"Your primary witness never implicated him."

"Right. Of course, *that* was a federal case. Is that the one you are interested in?"

Grove nodded but said, "Well, we really can't tell you that, as we have been saying."

"You'll have to go through channels, of course. Mark, is Captain Berman in his office this morning?"

Mark's head moved up slightly, and his shoulders moved, but he spotted Mason's hand, held lower than the top of his desk, his forefinger wagging back and forth. "No," Mark said. "I believe all the captains and the majors are enroute to a conference."

Mark raised his hands to his face and coughed into them.

"Need to go wash up," Mark said, and got up to go do so.

Grove grunted, and Orozco nodded, and they both left.

John muttered to himself, "You may be able to talk to him if the Braves game is rained out."

Mark peeked around the corner. "Are they gone?"

John nodded.

Mark came back to his desk. "Sorry I almost gave it away."

"'S okay. You recovered really well. And the way you worked in the conversation made it seem like you weren't a rookie detective. Building your credibility with the Feds is good."

John turned back to the paperwork he had been starting when the Bureau invaded. His eyebrows dropped. "Really good," he whispered.

"Something is still bothering me." Mark said when he had settled back in his chair.

Mason: "Was Elvis spotted at a 7-Eleven in Minneapolis?"

Alcalá: "Huh?"

Mason: "Post-nasal drip?"

Alcalá: "No!"

Mason: "Not enough raisins in your raisin bran?"

Alcalá: "Too many, actually, but that's not it, either."

Mason: "Need a sunnier parking space?"

Alcalá: "No way. I've lived here long enough to know what August will be like."

Mason: "My money was on Elvis. So, what's bothering you?"

"Where's the gunshot residue?" Mark asked. "At least part of the floor was hardwood, and if there was almost no residue on the body, a shot indoors like that should have left some on furniture, floor, or rug."

"There was that bit on the edge of the coffee table. It made

85

it look like the table was on the edge of the cone as the residue spread."

"So why wasn't there any on the Turkish rug?"

Mason nodded approval. "Was it cleaned up?"

"I don't think so, boss. GSR on rug would be impossible to clean up without at least leaving a trace of cleaner."

"Your point?"

"I've been over the forensics report. There 'no sich of a thing,' as Ado Annie would say."

"Trucks, stars, *and* Rogers and Hammerstein. The stuff we don't get in personnel folders."

"Come on, John, please? Can we stick to the subject?"

Mason nodded. "Sorry. Had extra coffee this morning. Yeah, I've thought of everything you mentioned. It only leads to one conclusion."

"Which is?"

"You tell me."

Alcalá's lips and eyebrows tensed in exasperation. "Why?"

Mason took a breath. "Look," he said, "I know I can seem silly or flippant, but this is training for you, Detective. Give me some thought here."

Alcalá closed his eyes for a couple of minutes. When he opened them, he said, "I don't know ... wait ... it wasn't cleaned up because it didn't touch the floor ... like there was something on the floor to catch it ... "

Mason nodded. "Good. Perhaps not 'to catch it,' but something that caught it, no matter what the original purpose was. Like a painter's drop cloth. And whatever it was bundled up and taken away."

"So, we're looking for a painter who moonlights as a hit man?"

"Well, a hit man who can work as a painter. But unless we find hard evidence that something was put down like that, it's just a guess." Mason stood up. "Come with me."

They trekked through six turns of hallway to the forensics offices. Welch's desk was unoccupied, but Lanny Johnson was riffling through some papers as they walked up.

"Hey Detective. Or is it Detectives?"

"Detectives," Mason said. "Lanny, this is my new guy, Mark Alcalá."

They shook hands.

"What can I do for you?" Johnson asked.

"We wanted to look at material and write-ups from the Bookman case. Can you help, or should we wait for Maddie?"

"I drew Sunday duty. But Mad showed me the index, and I can let you look at anything you want." Johnson used a nickname that wouldn't be heard if she were there.

"Index?"

"It's the paperless system we started using a few weeks ago. I think you missed the briefing. The master index is a drawing, a floor plan of the crime scene, divided into one-foot squares. The items in inventory are annotated with where in the grid things were found and which box things are stored in. There's still an alphabetical index as well."

"I didn't know about that either," Mason said. "Usually, I just ask Maddie, and she tells me what I want to know."

"Yeah, her memory is amazing. How do you want to do this?"

"Hmm. Are your indexes on paper or electronic?"

"They're PDFs. The originals are editable documents, but only those with special access get to those."

Alcalá said, "And we don't have access, right?"

87

Johnson nodded. "Right. And you won't get it."

Mason said, "Have you got a screen where we can look at them? And are the photos indexed to them as well?"

"Yes, on both counts. And we've gone all digital on the photos, except for special needs stuff, like infrared."

"You've made me a happy man, Johnson."

"Don't tell my wife. She'll be jealous."

Lanny pointed to a computer on a desk across the room. "Log in with your regular account, navigate to the Forensics folder, look for your case number under that. Indexes are at the top level. Just click wherever you want to look for something."

"Cool, thanks. Permissions?"

"Read only."

"Perfect."

The detectives sat in front of the computer.

"You drive," Mason said.

"Okay." Alcalá logged on and traipsed down the trail of folders.

"Where do I look?"

Mason said, "Start with the door jambs. Ballistics says the shooter was standing by the door to the kitchen, so start at that doorway and look at each one of the simplest paths to the outside doors."

"What am I looking for?"

"Anything out of place. Look at anything that plastic or cloth could catch on and see whether there's anything in the photos, or, better, physical evidence in the locations."

One spot on the index drawings after another, Alcalá clicked, and he and Mason looked over the reports. No residue had been found in kitchen, on the door frame, or the edge of the living room floor. Nothing.

Mason said, "Look in the inventory spreadsheet."

Alcalá clicked a few times.

"Search for scraps of plastic, thread, any stray material."

Alcalá searched for each of these in turn but found nothing.

Mason rapped his knuckles together. "Professional. Thorough. *Too* thorough."

"Hit man?"

"Naw. Contract killers get in, kill, get out, dispose of anything incriminating, and leave town. Their DNA isn't on file anywhere, and their fingerprints probably aren't. They don't care much about the evidence that's left at the scene, because it won't be connected to them."

"Then why all the attention to detail?"

Mason rapped his knuckles a couple more times.

"Because ... the killer is local. Did you smell paint at the scene?"

"No, I was too busy trying not to vomit."

Mason nodded.

"Search for paint."

The inventory showed a couple of cans of paint in the garage. The colors noted were not a match for the color of the living room.

Mason mused quietly. "So, he — assuming it's a man — let's say he's a painter. He's local, and he probably works for cash. No permits are required for painting, so there's not much chance someone will see him. And he's obsessively thorough. At least when he kills someone. At least."

2:00 p.m.

After Mason and Alcalá returned to their desks, Mason asked for the names from Nathan Bookman's address book.

"Here's the list." Mark handed John a copy of the list that he had given to Lieutenant Tejeda; an intern had transcribed all the information into a regular document.

John nodded thanks and scanned the list.

"And the Loo told me you were to divide the list with the Bureau guys according to your own discretion."

John, still scanning, nodded again.

"Got any ideas how you're going to split it up?"

"Yeah."

Grove and Orozco entered the squad room, wearing new nametags that allowed them unescorted access throughout the building.

"Let's find a conference room," John said. He led the agents and Mark down the hall. The large conference room was in use, so they went on to the small one. John and Orozco sat at the ends of the table, Mark and Grove on the sides.

"Okay," John said, "these are the interviews we have left to do." He handed them a copy of the list.

Everyone perused the list for a moment.

"So how do you want to divide this up?" Grove asked.

"In the interest of department budget, I was going to ask you guys to handle things south, and we'd concentrate on the people who live up here."

"That's mostly okay," Orozco said, "but we want to interview everyone associated with Kaiser Transceivers."

John narrowed his eyebrows and pursed his lips. "All right," he said, "here's how it plays out."

John took Orozco's copy of the list and circled all the names that were related to Kaiser and put a *K* next to each of them — a fourth of the entire list. Then he circled another fourth, choosing the farthest ZIP codes.

The agents nodded, promised daily write-ups, and said goodbye.

2:30 p.m.

John looked up at Mark absently. "Gotta run an errand. I'll be back in fifteen or twenty minutes."

"Okay."

John walked to his car and drove out of the parking lot. As he drove out, he dialed his phone.

"Ron, got a minute?"

Ron Penfield sounded surprised to hear from him. "Hey, John I have about ten, then I have guests arriving for a late Sunday dinner. What do you need?"

"I need you to go buy a prepaid cell phone. We'll swap the numbers later."

"Okay. Do I need MMS?"

"If you're okay with the extra expense, it couldn't hurt."

"Removable battery?"

"You read my mind."

After they rang off, John parked near a branch of his bank and turned off his phone, then opened the back cover and took out the battery. At the ATM, he withdrew a hundred dollars.

He reversed course, driving back past the station to the nearest Wal-Mart, bought a phone for cash, and stashed it in his trunk.

He reversed course again, driving back to his bank. In the parking lot, he reassembled his phone, powered it up and called Mark.

"I'm picking up a late lunch. Can I get you anything?"

"No, thanks. I had an early lunch."

John picked up a $1.29 hamburger at a drive through and headed back to his office. He stopped at the drink machine for a Diet Coke. At his desk he pulled the sandwich out and popped the top on his drink.

"Can I ask you a question?" Mark said.

"Sure." John's answer was muffled through white bread and beef.

"Is there a problem if I ask out someone who's involved in our case?"

"Who?"

"Ruth Sellers."

John shook his head. "No way. She was a close associate of the victim. The soonest you can go there is when the case is going to trial and neither side plans to call her as a witness. And after the trial would be better."

"So, there's no way? I mean, she didn't really know any-thing."

John drew a breath. "Let me look at the notes from your in-terview." He thumbed through the standing file until he found the correct pages.

"Lessee ... Ruth Sellers was on intimate terms with the victim, she took drives with him sometimes."

"Yeah. The fact that she was close to the victim means

the Assistant District Attorney — Has an ADA been assigned yet?"

Mark worked down through two memos to the one he wanted. "Heaton."

"Cora or Brock?"

"Cora. Are they related?"

"Husband and wife. Brock would bring in the victim's character and explore the characters of all his close associates weaving a story for the jury. Cora goes for the simplest case possible, evidence only, 'just the facts, officer.'"

"So, what's the message?"

"The message," John said, "is that Ruth Sellers is not likely to be called by the prosecution. There's no defendant yet, so we don't know what a defense attorney will do. Sellers said she occasionally drinks to excess, so her potential unreliability mitigates against her being called. If you were to establish this hypothetical relationship, my story will be that I told you not to. It'll be your badge on the line."

"I ought to think about it some more."

"Good idea."

8:03 p.m.

John and Ann's Tuesday lo mein had moved to Sunday this week — their shifting schedules mandated flexibility. John picked up the usual order on the way home and set it on the kitchen counter on his way in and collapsed into his recliner.

"Tough day?" his wife, Ann Fleming, asked.

"The most boring day ever," John said. "Non-stop paperwork on the Bookman case."

"Nate ... no, *Nathan* Bookman?"

John nodded.

Ann closed her eyes and thought. "Short. Curly hair in a mullet. Dressed like an urban cowboy. Was that him?"

John nodded again.

Before becoming a police officer and then a detective, John had been an electrical engineer at Kaiser Transceivers, a small defense firm. He had been one of the last three employees when the company closed, carrying all the leftover paperwork — even office supplies — into a secure warehouse facility in case something might be classified. That was just after the terrorist attacks of September 11, 2001. John's final paycheck was one of the company's last three financial transactions; the janitor and the computer system administrator who helped him move the boxes in got the other two.

Ann poured herself red wine and opened a bottle of Guiness for John. She beckoned him to come sit on the stools at the kitchen counter. They ate directly from the cartons, both using chopsticks — John had finally mastered the esoteric art after years of trying.

When John had eaten half his noodles and shrimp, Ann decided it was time.

"Lilia called me today."

John's face tightened and froze. His posture became rigid and defensive. Ann had said one of the things he never wanted to hear.

After a moment his eyelids thawed and blinked. He inhaled deeply and leaned into the back of his barstool, frozen for a full minute.

Finally, he released his breath and looked up in Ann's direction, seeing her unfocused in a circle of red.

"I told her to leave you the hell alone," John growled bitterly, throwing his chopsticks down.

Ann focused on his eyes and murmured, "It's not *me* you're trying to protect, John. It's yourself. And hiding yourself from your first wife and your daughter is *not* moving on with your life. At least not as an adult."

As she spoke, John gradually brought his wife into focus. His jaw remained tight as he glared. Finally, he brought himself back to the first commitment they had made to each other: honesty. As he examined her words and replayed in his mind every nuance of each syllable, he realized that was all she was doing.

John nodded, words not yet willing to migrate from his mind to his mouth.

As his anger and frustration settled, he picked up his chopsticks and poked at his lo mein without any enthusiasm.

Eventually — it seemed like years compressed into half a minute — he asked, "What did she want? And why did she call *you*?"

Ann thought for a minute before summarizing.

"She wants — no, she *needs* you to be a father. Not a mere ... financier. You have a *daughter*, John, and yes, an ex-wife. But Lilia can't be Adena's only parent."

"I wanted to be a parent with *you*," John said quietly. His face flushed and his lips quivered, both for just a moment.

Ann dabbed her own tears away with her napkin.

John took her nearer hand and held it as he looked into her eyes. At last, she nodded *I'm okay* and picked up her chopsticks. A sip of wine and she resumed eating.

John inhaled and fished more noodles and a shrimp from the carton. He chewed slowly. He swallowed and chased the food with a sip of his stout.

"I guess I can call her this week."

"Please," Ann said, "don't let this slip by."

Monday, June 25

At the county school system's network operations center, Grove and Orozco flagged down Carlton Donovan.

Servers hummed with the spin of disk drives and fans, and the ventilation system doubled the noise over everything else.

"Sorry about the noise," Donovan said loudly, "but I don't have a desk here — I'm filling in for the general manager while he's on vacation. I've got about ten minutes."

"It's no problem," Grove said just as loudly. "We're here to talk about Nathan Bookman. We're helping the county police with their investigation."

"Bookman? I think I saw him once after Kaiser shut down. That was a few years ago. I'm planning to go to the funeral, but mostly to see if I can say hello to any old Kaiser people."

"How well did you know him back then?"

"I was the IT administrator, so I met everyone who had a computer. When they had a problem, it was my job to fix it."

97

The fluorescent light was blinking overhead, so Donovan said, "Hold on a sec." He opened his day planner and added a note to the to-do list: *Call maint. about srvr rm lght.*

Orozco said, "So you worked on computers, including Bookman's, right?"

"Yeah."

"What can you tell me about his computing?"

"A little. I didn't work on the company projects; I was just the admin. As I understood it, he was the algorithm guy; he figured out how some of the stuff — encryption I think — was supposed to work, but he didn't write the software that went in the radios. Ron Penfield's group did that."

Grove asked a question, but he was too quiet to hear over the noise. Donovan turned his head and asked, "Could you repeat that?"

"Sorry," Grove said. "Did you have access to any of the classified work?"

"To be the admin, I had to have access to everything — Top Secret, Crypto, the whole thing. But my access was just as controlled as anyone's. When we got into the classified stuff, there were rules we had to follow for access: no one could bring in a cell phone or even a calculator; there was no Internet access in the secure network; you had to go through three security doors to get in, each with a different access method."

"Ever get audited?"

"Four times," Donovan said, "and we passed every security audit without a hitch."

Orozco said, "You mentioned someone — Ron ... Penfield. Tell me about him."

"What do you want to know? And because I'm curious, what does he have to do with the Bookman murder?"

"Look, you're not stupid," Grove said. "We're assisting the locals with the Bookman case and piggybacking our own Federal investigation onto it."

Donovan blinked a few times as he worked out the implications. "What do you want to know? I mean, Penfield and I haven't always gotten along. He was responsible for Kaiser going belly up."

One of Donovan's staff came by and dropped off some papers for signature.

"Did it ever seem like he had extra money?"

"No, not really. That was always Bookman. His cars were always something. He had this little MG, green, ran like a cheetah."

"Ever get to ride in it?"

"He gave me a ride when people went to lunch a couple of times."

"Back to Ron Penfield," Grove said. "Was he ever ... extra friendly with any of the female staff?"

"Or the male staff, for that matter?" Orozco added.

"No." Donovan answered so flatly the agents were stunned silent for a few seconds.

Donovan went on "He was always thoroughly devoted to his family. No exceptions. At any time. Ever."

"But he brought down the company. How?"

"From my perspective, it was because he subverted the C.M. system."

"C.M. ... Cable Modem?"

Donovan rolled his eyes. "Configuration Management. He made changes to system code on the radio we were working on, faked the configuration management records, reviews, everything. He was damned clever about it too; comments in the review process said just what the reviewers would have said. He understood how all the people on the project thought, or at least what they would say."

"Why did he do it?"

"He said there were technical problems that couldn't be overcome any other way."

Grove asked, "Would his changes have harmed the radio?"

"I wouldn't know. My job was just to keep the development and business systems running."

"How was he caught?"

"John Mason was the hardware guy; he was in a code review with the Army and spotted the changes."

Orozco cut in. "Detective Mason?"

"Yeah. He made it known to the customer, and that got the contract canceled. The company was shut down a few months later. Mason and I and one other guy actually carried boxes to a warehouse to be stored until they were destroyed."

Grove asked, "You mentioned you and Penfield didn't get along. Was it because the company shut down?"

"At first, yeah. I got a job with a dot-com while Kaiser was winding down. The money was really good, but when that went under, I was out of work and blamed Penfield for it. If Kaiser had stayed in business I probably would have stayed there."

"Are you still not getting along?"

"No, we're okay. We're not friends or anything, but I'm not mad anymore."

"Why the change?"

"Personal reasons."

1:00 p.m.

"Have you got all his credit card and bank records?"

"Six months' worth. Am I looking for anything in particular?"

"Electronics. Anyplace he could have bought a phone or a computer. It's inconceivable that he didn't have a computer or cell phone. The latter because he didn't have a land line."

Mark nodded. "So, I should ask for the receipts from the retailers and see what he actually bought."

"Yeah. Go for it."

After half an hour, Mark had a list of brick-and-mortar stores and online stores, with receipt numbers and dates. He started calling them and spent the next couple of hours calling until he finally said "Bingo!"

"Whatcha got?" Mason asked.

"He bought a computer — top of the line — from Alienware in March."

"High end gaming?"

Mark nodded. "And when they asked about warrants and reasons and stuff, and I told them he was murdered and the computer was missing, they said fax them the warrant and they'll give me some more information the techies might be able to use to track it down."

Mason nodded. "Hardware address of the Ethernet circuit, prolly."

"That sounds like what they said. But I don't understand."

"Every network device has a unique address that's accessible to the router it's talking through. If the computer is hooked up through a public network, we can get a warrant to have them to 'listen' for a connection from that device. They call us and we investigate."

"But I thought the address was changeable."

"That's the logical address, layered on top of the physical address. It's used for talking to the computer on a different level. Think of the hardware address as non-verbal communication and the logical address as verbal. It's not really like that, but that's the quality of the separation."

"Are there any weaknesses?"

"Sure. The new user might not go through a public hookup. Behind a residential gateway, say, we'd never see it. Or he might go through a VPN — a virtual private network, with encryption to a central server somewhere. Also, even the hardware address can be spoofed if you have the technical chops. And that assumes the murderer didn't just throw the computer away."

"So, it's a long shot?"

"Yeah, but it's what we've got. Get one of the rookies to run the errands for you. You keep calling stores."

"Why?"

"We still don't have a phone. Like I already said, without a land line, there's not a reasonable way he didn't have a cell phone. Also, call Internet phone providers like Vonage and see if he had an account."

"He could have had a prepaid phone."

"Yeah, but we need to check everything."

Mark nodded, resigned. There's no glamor in being thorough.

Hours and dozens of phone calls later, Mark was talking with a customer service person from an online electronics store.

He noted the name of the woman he was talking to so he

could converse on-to-one, and he explained who he was and why he was calling.

"Can you track a specific receipt for me? ... Yes. Okay here's the number." He rattled off a string of letters and digits. "That's right. Okay, I just need a listing of what was on the order ... uh huh ... can you give me the EIMI number? You're right, it's IMEI. Or is it EIEIO? ... Sorry, I've just been on the phone for three hours tracking retail purchases ... Okay, shoot."

He wrote down a string of letters and numbers longer than the receipt number. "Okay, and is this a CDMA phone or a GSM phone? I see. Okay, thanks ... I really appreciate your help Adena."

Mason swiveled around as Mark hung up and stared at him for ten full seconds.

Mark was unaware of this because he was turned slightly away as he finished entering the information into his computer.

Mason turned away as Mark turned toward him.

"I have a lead on a cell phone purchase. It's a GSM ..." Mark saw Mason's lips were pressed together and his jaw was trembling. "Are you okay, John? You're pale as a Norwegian from Milwaukee after a long winter."

"I'll be fine," Mason said through clenched teeth. "Go on."

"It's a GSM phone, top of the line, purchased outright without a contract. Do you want me to keep going through retailers or try to get a line on which phone company activated it?"

Mason relaxed a little and closed his eyes. "Hit the phone companies next, then finish the stores when you have what they can give you."

Mark nodded and pulled his list of cell phone carriers.

Mason inhaled and said, "You're right; I'm not feeling well.

I'm going home. Get some help calling retailers. You call the cell service providers, and when you're done with that, go back and help mop up the retail."

"Okay. Get better."

Mason nodded and left.

4:07 p.m.

At home, Mason didn't take any medicine or lie down. Instead, he made a cup of pungent herbal tea and changed into hospital scrubs. In a dark, sparsely furnished room in a back corner of the house, he lit two candles on opposite walls and took up a lotus position on a mat facing a third, blank wall, halfway between the candles.

He was still sitting that way when Ann got home over an hour later. She noticed the teacup, which was now empty, leaves sitting in the bottom; the aroma of tea and candles permeated the room.

She saw his position and changed into her own scrubs, pulled her dark brown hair into a short ponytail, and sat beside him.

After half an hour more, he stirred and sighed.

She put a hand on his and asked, "What happened, babe?"

He closed his eyes and convulsed slightly, and said, "Today Mark was making some phone calls. He's pretty good on the phone. At the end of each call, he thanked the person who helped him by name. The last person he talked to before I left was a woman named Adena."

Ann caught the corner of her mouth between her teeth for a moment. "I'm so sorry, babe. It's hard. I'm not experiencing it the way you are, but I know it hurts. How about we hit a drive through and find a shade tree to eat under."

"You know how to soothe the beast. Okay."

Ann put out the candles while John took his teacup to the kitchen. A few minutes later they were out the door, still wearing scrubs and shod in flip-flops.

It wasn't lo mein night, so they wound up with fish and fries and large paper cups of iced tea, John's unsweetened and Ann's half-and-half.

They settled in a park near their home, seated in the grass in the shade of an enormous oak tree. Still an engineer at heart, John settled them on the leading edge of the shade, so that as the sun progressed, they would remain in the shadow for at least an hour.

They began eating in silence. Finishing the last bite of his first plank of fish, John said, "I guess I've ..."

Ann waited.

"I've been a terrible father."

He sipped some tea.

"Not terrible," Ann said. "You were never abusive; you never made unreasonable demands —"

"*Any* demands," John interrupted, "except to leave you alone." He waggled a fry between thumb and forefinger.

"Which may have been too much. But you never failed to make child support or alimony."

"So, I could have been worse." John closed his eyes and shook his bowed head back and forth. "That still doesn't make up for what I *should have been.* But if I had been *that,* you and I wouldn't be here now."

"You've made an amazing discovery," Ann said with just a hint of playfulness. "You can't change the past. Wow!"

John couldn't help the corners of his mouth turning up. "I guess Steve Miller was right. So, what's my path forward, doc?"

Ann replied succinctly. "Feel what you're feeling; feel it fully; don't cut it off too early. But keep an eye on the future; know where you're going. This will keep you from being captive to the guilt feelings, from being debilitated by it."

"How long will this take?"

"Who knows? There's not a fixed timeline; you just have to walk through it."

Tuesday, June 26

Mason was usually the one who called people to the interview room. This time, his presence was requested. Required, actually. He guessed it would have been demanded had he balked. Or they would have gone over his head to get him ordered to appear.

The interviewers were the FBI agents, Grove and Orozco.

Orozco, seated to Mason's right, led off. "Detective. Can we call you John?"

Mason looked at him and nodded once. He hoped the agent didn't notice the corner of his mouth twitching. This would be fun.

"John, I know you're stonewalling us on the Bookman case. We're not leaving here until I know why."

Evidently, Orozco was playing Bad Cop. Mason decided to play hurt and dumb.

"What do you mean, Vic?"

Grove, standing in the corner, frowned. Mason hadn't asked to use their first names. And they knew he had only heard Orozco referred to as Victor.

Mason went on. "I've given you every bit of evidence; you will be there when we open his safe for the first time. You've been invited by the department to participate in the investigation. What am I missing?"

"What you're missing, John, is that we want this case." Orozco pointed at Mason and stared into his eyes. "Your department has discretion in the investigation, and we think the reason they're holding it so tightly is you!"

"Vic," Grove said, "slow down. John's not trying to obstruct anything. Like he said, we've got access, and we can help him out, too."

Good cop, Mason thought. *I was wondering when Rufus would pop up.*

Mason said, "And you haven't shown Federal authority. All you have to do is show the requirement to me or someone in my chain of command and everything, absolutely everything, is yours as fast as I can hand it off. Can you explain your claim of jurisdiction?"

Orozco changed the subject. "You worked with Bookman at Kaiser Transceivers. That was, what? Eight years ago?"

"Just under seven. How do you know about that?"

Orozco ignored his question. "How well did you know him when you worked there?"

"It wasn't a big company, so everyone knew everyone else. And we were on the same program anyhow. I was the lead hardware designer; Book was the crypto algorithm guy."

"And have you seen him or had any contact with him since?"

Mason shook his head. "No, I haven't."

Grove said, "You said 'crypto algorithm,' not 'crypto software.' Who was the software lead?"

"That was Ron Penfield. Book couldn't code his way to the mouth of a cave if it was bright and sunny outside."

Grove snickered.

"Ron's on your interview list," Mason said.

Grove was holding a manila folder; he consulted it and nodded to Orozco.

"Wait a second," Mason said. "I never saw Bookman, but he was peripherally mentioned in a case I worked last Fall, but he was never an active POI."

"And just what case was that?"

"I mentioned it the other day: The death of the senator, Charles Jamison."

"Oh," Grove said, "that was you."

"Well, our department was involved, if that's what you mean."

"No, John, it was *you*, not anyone else."

Mason experienced a moment of relief at having kept Ron Penfield from being recognized as part of the case. He decided to throw them a bone to see who'd chew. "Are you guys following up on the Jamison case? He was supposed to have influenced some defense contracts."

"Yes," Grove said too quickly, "he did do that. Do you know whether Bookman was involved in any of that?"

"The prosecutor's lead witness has refused to name him. One of Bookman's cars — one like it, anyway — was seen with the witness, but only one person places Bookman in the case. But you know all this already."

Orozco snorted. "Of course we know it. But are you holding anything back from the prosecutor's people?"

"Not a thing. Once it became about the Senator, I was a cooperator, not a leader. Of course, the real question ... never mind."

"What? What's the question?"

"Why wasn't the Bureau involved to start with? You've never given me a simple confirmation about what you're working on."

"That's classified," Grove cut in.

Orozco wheeled around and looked at his partner. "Rob!"

Mason smiled. "In ordinary society, people use *classified* just to mean a closely held secret. But to the federal government, it means something particular."

"He already knows," Grove said, nodding toward Mason.

Orozco looked back at Mason, the question lining his forehead.

Mason nodded. "Yep."

The agents exhaled in relief.

Mason said, "As for classified, I was Top Secret with crypto as well. But you knew that."

Grove tapped his cheekbone. "If you know what division we're from, you know what conclusions to draw. How about this: You keep the lead on the Bookman case, keep us up to date, and we continue to assist."

"But no more secrets, like holding onto the knowledge about the safe," Orozco said.

"It's a deal."

Mason left the room, closing the door behind him.

Grove said, "Thanks for following in on the suggestion."

"No problem, but why aren't we forcing jurisdiction? It's just a couple of signatures."

"Because we can't take over without becoming too visible,

and remember: Mason is a POI. This lets us stay close to him."

10:47 a.m.

"So, what do you want with me?" Ron Penfield asked.

He sat at his desk at Armstrong High School, across from the FBI agents. The blinds on his windows were open, letting in what light was available on a cloudy day.

"We're assisting the local police with their investigation of the Bookman case," Orozco said. "I was wondering whether you had heard about that."

"Of course, his death was in the paper, and the police investigation was mentioned. But I haven't seen Nathan for years. Looks like I missed my chance."

"We understood you worked with Nathan Bookman at Kaiser Transceivers. What can you tell me about his work there?"

Ron took a sip of coffee. He had offered coffee to the agents from the office coffee maker (Ron's own coffee had come from home in a vacuum bottle); Grove had accepted, but Orozco was carrying a bottle of water. "Book was the crypto algorithm guy. He wrote algorithms in bad Fortran, we converted them to C and got them to work on the radio we were working on."

"What kind of radio was it?"

"Highly classified. You've got to talk to the Department of the Army to learn about that. My clearance is gone, and it has been for seven years. After the program was shut down, we all got debriefed and I don't have any insight into where the Army's program went, if anywhere."

"Why?" Grove asked.

"Because that's the way classified programs work. Or, in this case, don't work."

"No," Grove said, "I mean why was the Kaiser program shut down?"

Ron closed his eyes and took a deep breath. "I'll bet you already know that. To get the radio to succeed, I had to rewrite some of the executive software in ways that violated the contract. When it was discovered, I was fired, then the contract was taken away from the company, then the company went under."

"You weren't prosecuted?" Orozco asked.

Ron pulled his lips back between his teeth; his eyebrows pulled down and pushed his eyes closed, holding tears back; he exhaled and didn't inhale for half a minute.

"I hurt a lot of people," he said, eyes still closed. "A lot of friends. But I wasn't prosecuted. I believe there was some contemplation of a civil suit brought by the government, but it never materialized."

Finally, he opened his eyes and asked, "But what does this have to do with Bookman's murder? As I said, I haven't seen him for years."

Orozco said, "We're involved because we think Bookman had extra income that was not legal. Income related to government contract work."

Ron's eyes went to the ceiling. "But it's not primarily about the money," he said. "If it were, you'd be from the Treasury Department. It's not related to the Jamison prosecutions; if it were, someone from the Federal prosecutor's office would be here. That doesn't leave much that I would have any knowledge of except his algorithm work at Kaiser." He focused on Orozco. "Is that it?"

"Okay," Orozco said, "I'll answer: Yes. And we think someone was paying him for off-the-books encryption work."

"Who?"

"Who do *you* think?" Grove asked.

"Could be anyone. Could be privacy nuts with cash; most of those don't have that much cash, but if one did ... well, you get the idea. Some of them are anarchists; that might be the FBI angle. Could have been organized crime; that's got FBI all over it. As does the involvement of foreign governments."

Grove looked at Orozco. "This guy's pretty bright."

Orozco said, "We may be investigating one of those lines of thought."

"Or we may not," Grove added. "But since Kaiser shut down, you've done pretty well."

"You mean you know I have a couple of mutual funds in seven digits," Ron said. "A couple of stocks, too."

"Close to eight digits," Grove said. "In both funds."

"If you look back far enough — and I can document this if you want, down to the penny — you'll see that I inherited some money from my dad — my mom died the year before he did — and I invested it. I got a good tip on a stock owned by one of those funds that went up and still goes up. Everything is completely above board."

"What about the foundation?" Grove demanded.

"Foundation ... oh you mean the trust. I put some of the money aside to help people who didn't come out as well as I did after the Kaiser shutdown."

Grove's voice began to rise. "And how many people have you helped?"

"I don't know. I don't administer the fund or even get reports." Ron's voice rose to match Grove's. "I don't know

113

how many. I don't know who. I don't know how much."

Even louder, Grove asked, "Is the money just going to sit there forever?"

"No! When the ten-year anniversary hits, all the remaining funds go to a couple of charities." Ron began to turn red.

"*I don't believe you!*" Grove was shouting. "There is no way you are so above board that you're practically levitating, Penfield. You have *not* seen the last of us."

Grove stormed out with Orozco at his heels.

11:32 a.m.

"John, I don't like it."

Ron and Mason spoke on their prepaid phones.

"Relax, Ron. This is the reason they came after you. How much did they know?"

"They knew enough about Kaiser before it shut down."

"What did they ask about?"

"They asked about Bookman, about what I did in relation to his work, about why ..." Ron nearly gasped it out: "... about why Kaiser shut down."

Ron took a breath before continuing.

"About my personal finances since then. They knew I've done okay; they knew about the trust; they knew I could account for everything to the penny."

"And?"

"And they accused me of ..." Ron's voice was rising.

"Of what?"

"Of *hiding* something."

"It was a tactic, a technique to get you to do something — anything. A lot of people — a lot who have real money, anyway — don't have finances as squeaky clean as yours. Look at it from their point of view. Since being fired, you've grown rich, way north of the ninety-ninth percentile."

"So?"

"So, they think there may be money flowing under the table somewhere. You may be spending it; you may be receiving it. They don't know, but they have to look at it. And if you react, they'll keep following you until something turns up. If you carry on as usual, they will have to start looking elsewhere."

"So, I ignore them?" Ron was calming down, slowly.

"Yep. Don't be surprised if they put surveillance on you. They like to put rookies on that. And we will have to be careful even about using these phones. Take the battery out of your regular phone when we're talking on this channel. And don't call from your car anymore."

"Do they have the resources for something like that?"

"Let me give you a hint," Mason said. "Grove and Orozco aren't from white collar crimes; they aren't investigating corruption charges."

"There's no kidnapping, no bank robbery ... oh."

"Yeah, 'oh.' Counter intel."

"So ..." Ron said, "they were working Bookman as a foreign agent."

"That's the way I see it. I don't know what else they have, but if they're talking to you, it doesn't seem likely they have much to go on."

"What can you tell me about the case — Bookman's murder, I mean."

"There are two things I haven't worked out yet," Mason

115

admitted. "First one is the lack of forensic evidence. No hairs, almost no gunshot residue, nothing."

"What happened with the residue?"

"Book was shot inside his house with a small-caliber firearm, a .22. Forensics says it was probably a handgun. The body wasn't moved; he was inside; but there wasn't any GSR on the floor in the room or from any shooting position in the house."

"Weird," Ron observed. "Does it seem like the site was cleaned up after the fact?"

"No. There was a trace of gunshot residue on the edge of the coffee table. A professional crime scene cleaner — legitimate or not — would have gotten that."

"Wonder how they managed that."

"You and me both."

12:02 p.m.

"What can our department do for the Bureau today?" Captain Berman stood to shake the hands of the FBI agents, Grove and Orozco.

Grove said, "As you are probably aware, we have an interest in the Bookman case."

"Sure. Your presence was noted in the crime scene access log. And Mason has reported that you have cooperated and respected the boundaries we asked for."

"Certainly, we have no intention of impeding the investigation. In fact, our idea is quite the opposite."

"What kind of help is the Bureau offering?"

Grove's lips twitched. "We would like to take over the case."

" 'Take over'?"

"Yes, Captain."

"Is there a problem with the way we are handling it?"

"No, everything has been very good. Your crime scene unit is one of the best we have seen."

Orozco nodded agreement.

"I'll be sure to pass that along," Berman said. "Welch and her crew will be pleased to hear it. But what, exactly, makes this a federal case? There's been no kidnapping, no bank robbery, no evidence that *we* have to indicate a state line was crossed. Nathan Bookman was not a government employee at any level. What puts this in your jurisdiction?"

Orozco finally spoke. "Captain — that's so formal. May I call you Frank?"

Berman nodded and sniffed and avoided smiling. He knew the *I'm your friend* routine as well as anyone.

"Frank, we have a major case running involving a serious Federal crime, and we have indications that Bookman was involved. I'm sure you've spoken with Mason, so you know our interest."

Berman flared his nostrils a couple of times. "I'm afraid, then, that I can't turn the case over to you. Until you can *show* that you have clear jurisdiction, I can't even consider this becoming your case. I know that Mason has been giving you copies of all the evidence — transcripts, reports, whatever. You're welcome to that, and we will continue to keep you up to date. You will need to keep in touch through Lieutenant Sergio Tejeda."

He scribbled the name and number on the back of one of his own cards and pushed it across the desk.

"I must protest this, Frank," Orozco said. "Besides providing schedule and budgetary relief —"

117

"Your protest is noted," Berman cut in. "But again, unless you provide clear evidence that this is really your case after all, I must reject your request."

He wrote on the back of another business card.

"If this is not satisfactory, you can take it up with Major Rusher."

Berman pushed the second card across his desk, and watched with amusement as the agents untangled their legs from the scant space and left.

He pushed an autodial button on his desk phone. A tinny, nasal, female voice sounded through the speaker. "Major Rusher's office."

Berman picked up the handset. "Helen, this is Frank Berman. Could I talk to Brian?"

1:04 p.m.

Mason arrived at his desk, but before sitting down, he planned his assault on the four-inch stack of paper for the Bookman case.

First up was the Medical Examiner's report, which confirmed that the victim was in good health. Except for the fatal gunshot wound.

Preliminary toxicology showed low levels of an over-the-counter antihistamine in his bloodstream, and the autopsy revealed slight inflammation of the sinuses.

"He had a cold," John muttered to himself.

Finally, there was no evidence the body was moved after death.

Next up came the draft of the forensics report, including

the appendix that revealed the presence of the safe.

Mason already knew the scene surrounding the body was nearly free of gunshot residue. Trace amounts, invisible to the eye, were found on the top and along edge of the coffee table. The radius around the body was checked, including lines of sight that led into two other rooms (the kitchen and the hallway), and there was no more residue. At all. Not even a little.

All the latent fingerprints belonged to either Bookman or to one of the two women who cleaned his house twice a week.

Mason picked up his phone and dialed.

"Welch."

"Hey, Maddie, John. Got a second?"

"Sure, John. What do you need?" Welch sounded totally zapped.

"When you were doing Bookman's house, did you check all around the door jambs going into the hall and the kitchen?"

"Yep. And the coat closet just inside the hall — the door opens so you can see inside from the living room."

"Meaning someone in the closet could see into the living room as well. And it was all clean."

"You got it. We checked the outside door, too. Anything else?"

"One more thing: Did you get a look inside the wall around the safe yet?"

"My guys ... wait a second."

Mason heard Welch shuffling papers.

"Here it is. Sorry it didn't make the draft. Yes, the wall was checked on all four sides as well as the wall of the room behind — the home office. No funny business: No wiring or cameras, no microphones or anything."

Mason exhaled. "So, nothing to indicate the safe is under an extra layer of surveillance. How much did that put me back?"

"Oddly, we were able to do that within scope the day of. The truck had the new snake camera on it, and Roberto was itching to use it. Is there anything else?"

"Not right now, thanks."

Mason hung up and looked at the next report.

A plainclothes officer had interviewed the cleaning ladies. Both women were Mexican, and all their immigration papers were in order. They rarely saw Nathan Bookman; his payment to their bank account was electronic.

They cleaned Bookman's house on Tuesday and Friday. Nothing was amiss on their last visit. They liked working for Bookman: They normally arrived at his house in the middle of the morning, and he let them watch Telemundo on the big-screen TV while they ate lunch. Back in December, he paid them for Christmas — it was a Tuesday — even though they didn't work that day.

One of them, the younger one, said the king-sized bed sometimes looked like more than one person was sleeping in it, but neither of them had ever seen anyone at the house but the owner.

DMV and property records showed Bookman owned his house and cars outright.

A progress report from the plainclothes officer checking communications channels confirmed Bookman had no telephone land line — not common, but becoming more so. He had an account with one of the cell phone companies for its maximum data plan. Internet came through his cable company, and he used a few gigabytes of data each month. His TV cable was subscribed to the full range of pay channels.

Usage records were being gathered by the providers and would be turned over to the police when their respective court orders came through. The court orders were on the judge's desk and would be signed today.

Mason nodded. Everything was satisfactory, except for two things: The paucity of forensic evidence, and the complete lack of phones and computers.

Mason's phone rang. On the other end was the Ribo Security installation manager who had overseen the installation of Bookman's safe. They planned to meet at Bookman's house at three thirty p.m.

2:00 p.m.

Just as Mason rang off, Mark Alcalá walked in and said, "The Bookmans are here. I keep wanting to say 'Bookmen'. Should I put them in the conference room?"

"Naw, bring them back here."

While Mark fetched Nathan Bookman's parents, John arranged a couple of chairs so they could interact comfortably.

After they were seated, James Bookman said, "Detective, I know that it takes time to find a murderer in a case like this, but we need to be able to get back home to work as soon as possible."

Joyce added, "And we want to take possession of his house and property at your *earliest convenience* as well."

"Of course," John said. "We don't want to hold on to anything any longer than absolutely necessary. I was just looking over the medical examiner's report, and there's no doubt that the coroner will declare this a murder. I understand the funeral is planned for tomorrow afternoon."

Joyce asked, "What was the cause of death? Was it the gunshot you told us about?"

"Yes, ma'am. Nathan was killed by a .22-caliber hollow-point bullet to the forehead."

She asked, "Will you be able to identify the gun when you have it?"

"No, dear," James said. "When the bullet hit his skull, it began to expand like a mushroom and tore a hole the diameter of a nickel through his brain before it broke into pieces."

Joyce blanched and trembled when her husband described the damage done to her son's body.

"That's not quite right," John said. "The bullet did expand, but it didn't break up. There are still striations on the base of the bullet, — Mark!" Mason had finally seen Joyce's reaction.

"Eh?" Mark said.

"Get Mrs Bookman some water!"

Mark brought a bottle of water and a clean plastic cup. He started to offer it to James, then thought better of it and opened the bottle and poured the water himself. John took the cup from Mark and handed it to her.

She sipped and took a couple of minutes to recover. James shifted uneasily until Mason continued.

"The base of the bullet is brass, so the marks there can be linked to a particular firearm if it is found. The chances of that are not good in this case, I'm afraid."

"Why not?"

"Because there was almost no trace evidence at the scene. The gun — likely a handgun — was not at the scene. There was no residue on Nathan's body or clothing, so he didn't kill himself."

"And he wasn't killed at close range," James said. "Isn't that right?"

"Just so."

"Was his body moved to where it was found?"

"No, it was not moved at all."

James said, "That's nonsense. He was shot in an enclosed space and there is no residue anywhere?" Mason heard the "*CSI* effect" cutting in.

"There was a little on the edge of the coffee table," Mark said. "We don't understand it now, but we will figure it out."

James asked, "Was this a professional killing? A 'hit'?"

Joyce's hand quaked again, and a few drops spilled from the water cup onto the skirt of her suit.

Mason said, "We're open to that possibility, but we haven't reached a conclusion. When you arrived here, we were just about to go to Nathan's house to open his safe."

"Did you find the combination?"

"Well, no, this is a two-key safe. We have both keys, and a representative of the security company will be there. You are welcome to join us if you like."

James said, "Let's go, dear."

3:32 p.m.

Mason and Alcalá arrived at the crime scene, followed by Mr and Mrs Bookman. Joyce was quiet but seemed to have regained her composure.

While they waited inside the house for the security company's representative to arrive, the FBI agents knocked on the open front door.

Mason introduced the agents to the Bookmans.

James asked what their interest in the case was, but they were as evasive with the victim's parents as they had been with the police.

Mason asked the agents to come by the station later to pick up the updated reports.

When the security consultant arrived, he introduced himself as Alton Williams. He brought his own set of keys for the safe. "We're fully bonded," he explained. "At the customer's discretion we may keep a set of keys or, for a dial or digital safe, a copy of the combination."

"Why are there two keys?" Mason asked.

"The idea is for the customer to keep the two keys in separate places, so that if one is found by a burglar, say, he won't be able to get inside. And even with both keys, they have to be used in the correct order or the safe remains locked."

"So, it's like a safe deposit box. Is it left, then right?" Alcalá asked.

"It's written down here. We choose the first key randomly — with a coin flip at installation time, actually — and make the adjustment when the installation's being done."

Grove and Orozco hung back, letting everyone else have the close view.

Williams asked for the police paperwork, and Alcalá supplied it. Williams made a roster of the people present, saying "Our insurance company requires this," and each of them initialed it.

Once open, the contents of the safe proved exceedingly ordinary. There were two shelves, both containing the humdrum paperwork any homeowner might have: Home deed, car titles, insurance policies, and a note directing the reader to Nathan's lawyer to obtain a copy of his will.

Williams revealed no interest in the contents of the safe, but he examined the safe itself. "It appears secure and unaltered," he said, though his eyebrows lowered slightly.

"Mark," Mason said, "Would you take Mr and Mrs Bookman to the dining room — there's room to spread out there — to look over the papers?"

Alcalá gathered the documents, the parents, and the Bureau agents and went through.

When they had cleared the room, Mason asked Williams, "What's worrying you?"

"I'm not sure. We sell a lot of these; they're secure and relatively inexpensive. I provide the final delivery paperwork after the installation is complete, and we look over the safe itself pretty thoroughly. Something's not quite right here, but I can't put my finger on it."

Nodding, Mason said, "Change of plans. You keep the keys; the bond is still on."

"Not a problem for me."

Mason handed him a card. "If you realize what's bothering you, no matter when, day or night, call my cell phone. If I don't answer, leave a message to call you back, but no details. This is important: Give the details only to me — no one else."

"Yes, Detective."

7:17 p.m.

At home that night, Mason was telling Ann about his day. Even though it had only been two days since last week's delayed lo mein night, they were eating Chinese carryout straight from the paper cartons.

"The husband, James, is an unfeeling schlemiel," John said.

Ann said, "Yiddish?"

John nodded. "He described the gunshot like he was talking to his hunting buddies about taking down a rabid dog. He was talking about his *son*. He paid no attention, had no consideration for his wife's feelings. Just belted out what was on his mind. His *wife* was there, and he ignored her feelings, damn him."

"What a brute," Ann said. "The wife — what's her name?"

"Joyce."

"Is she better?" Ann asked.

"No. No, she's not. I mean, she's willing to shame her son publicly for what she calls his sexual misconduct. It's no wonder Bookman — Nathan, I mean — laughed to them about his girlfriends. If they were my parents, I'd want to rub it in, too."

Ann put their chopsticks and wine glasses in the dishwasher. "You aren't usually this agitated," she said. "I think you should hit the mat before going to sleep."

John dropped the cartons in the trash can. "Yeah," he said. "I think you're right."

Wednesday, June 27

5:30 a.m.

Ron Penfield rose much earlier than usual. The little sleep he had achieved had been light and not at all restful, so he finally gave up and got up. The interview (*the interrogation,* he thought) wouldn't leave his thoughts.

He tried reading. Tried TV. Tried sitting and staring into the void. Nothing helped.

Finally, about six thirty, he decided to shower. Maybe the warm water flowing over his body would help him relax. If he was drowsy afterward, he'd email the school office and tell them he wouldn't be in. They'd know how to rearrange his appointments.

Ron turned on the shower and got a drink from the sink, then tossed his pajamas in the hamper.

Standing under the falling water didn't help. He adjusted the temperature four times. No relaxation.

Finally, he took the shampoo bottle and held it for a minute. After he pushed the cap on one side to open it, he flipped the bottle over to actually dispense some shampoo into his hand. Before any came out, the bottle slipped from his hand and fell on the floor of the shower. The bottle didn't break, but he swore at his own clumsiness and bent over to pick it up.

He finished his hair without further incident, but when he grabbed the soap bar to lather up, it slid out of his hand to the floor. The soap was unharmed, but his attitude worsened at the sight of the corner flattened by the fall to the tile floor.

He figured he wouldn't be able to sleep. After he got out and dried off, he sent an email to Dr B and went to sit in his home office. At least there, if he didn't get anything done, he wouldn't be in anyone's way.

9:32 a.m.

At his desk, Mason sighed audibly and dialed his phone. When Williams answered the phone at Ribo Security, the detective said hello, then went on. "Yesterday, you said something seemed off about Nathan Bookman's safe. Have you been able to figure out what was wrong?"

"No, Detective. I'm not even sure there was anything to notice. It was just a feeling I got. Like I said, we install a lot of this model. It's relatively inexpensive, but it offers good fire protection, and it's easily built into a wall that's only a couple of inches thicker than normal."

"Yeah, just deep enough for folded papers." Mason thanked him and rang off.

2:15 p.m.

Ron Penfield arrived about fifteen minutes before the funeral was to start, and he greeted John Mason, who was sitting on the back pew. The funeral was being held in the funeral home's chapel, and a reception would be held afterward in a larger, open room.

Ron and John were the only people in the chapel so far.

Ron asked, "Is that your big truck sitting half a block up Clifford Gray?"

"You spotted it, huh?" John said. "Yeah, that's ours. In addition to my guys, the FBI people are in there."

"I told you I met them the other day. Have they told you why they're interested?"

"It's what we already discussed. And they're sending signals that they're about to demand jurisdiction."

They heard a low-pitched rumble and felt the building vibrating slightly. Both glanced at the outside wall that was nearest the parking lot.

They looked up at men entering the room. One was dressed in a black suit and black shirt, the other wore a black racing jacket and expensive sunglasses.

"Later," John said. "Gotta check the comms."

Ron nodded, then moved to the center of a pew on the right side of the room in about the middle row. Several more men and women entered, but they didn't seem to be together.

The first two men who entered the room had remained standing, talking to each other as others entered, but now the one in the racing jacket sat next to Ron on the aisle. He stuck a hand out.

"Tim Farmer."

Farmer was about five feet, eight inches, possessed rounded features and curly brown hair cut to business length.

"Ron Penfield. How did you know Nathan?"

"Book? We were in the Pantera car club together. You?"

"Used to work together a long time ago. How often did you see him?"

"We had meetings four times a year — middle Monday of each quarter."

Cheap, recorded organ music began to play.

"Bad presets on the B3," Farmer said. "And worse speakers to play it through."

More people were entering as they talked. Ron's eyebrows went up.

"Electric organ. The presets they're using were chosen poorly."

Ron said, "Car club, huh? Bookman always loved his cars. I think it's starting. Are you staying for the reception?"

Farmer nodded, then both turned their attention to the front.

A minister entered, a short, round, middle-aged man with slick hair, followed by a couple who looked to be in their early sixties, both wearing black. They sat on the pew just in front of the lectern.

A moment later the final chords sounded from the organ and the minister moved to the reading stand and began.

"I'm so happy to be here with you," he said, smiling.

Ron rolled his eyes. It was fixing to be *that* kind of service.

The minister launched into an extended, heartwarming story from his boyhood and a loss he experienced and recovered from. When that one was done, he told another story he said was from late the previous year. Somewhere in the middle, he made an oblique reference to a Bible verse; Ron recognized it was out of context. Way out.

Near the end of the second story, the minister started to cry.

Farmer leaned over to Ron and whispered, "My mom goes to this guy's church. She loves him. When I visited at Easter he told the same story word for word, including tears on the very same syllable."

Ron acknowledged with a shrug and a raised eyebrow and went on listening.

The minister then asked if anyone would like to say anything "in remembrance of the deceased." Ron realized that at no time had the minister used Nathan Bookman's name.

Bookman's father got up and said he supposed everyone knew that he and his son didn't get along, but that he loved him and would miss him anyway. His mother sat stone-still.

The minister asked, "Would anyone else care to share?"

Silence.

"Anyone at all?" He looked at each person in the room individually.

More silence.

"Going ... going ... gone. Let's pray." He then prayed briefly.

A man in a suit led the couple from the front row away. The funeral director mentioned that there would be a receiving line in the parlor just down the hall.

Ron bowed his head, looking at the floor to try to suppress his anger. Farmer glanced at Ron and decided not to try to talk to him.

2:50 p.m.

In the receiving line, Ron found himself standing between two women who only acknowledged each other's presence by facing exactly away from each other. As a consequence, they both had their backs to him.

The woman ahead of him was tall — in heels she was taller than Ron — and had short blond hair. Her shoulders were so broad and level that had this been the nineteen eighties, he would have assumed she wore shoulder pads in her suit.

The woman behind him was average height with long, long brown hair; her close-fitting dress — rather like a cocktail dress or party dress with an extra underlay to add modesty — narrowed her shoulders and hips but allowed some expression for her generous bustline.

The line moved quickly and in only a few minutes Ron was expressing his condolences to James and Joyce Bookman.

Joyce asked, "How did you know our son?"

"We worked together at Kaiser Transceivers," Ron said. "Nathan was a genius at the kind of mathematics our project required."

"That was a nasty business when the company folded," James said. "Do you know what happened? Nathan only told us that someone did something the government didn't like."

Ron felt the blood leaving his face. He was trying to form words when the woman in line behind him introduced herself as Ruthie Sellers and proceeded to monopolize the conversation. Grateful, Ron slipped away into the middle of the room and looked around.

In addition to John Mason, Ron recognized half a dozen

people from his days at Kaiser.

Carlton Donovan was talking to Nolan McCloskey. As Ron approached them, McCloskey spun on one heel and stepped away. Ron shook Donovan's hand and asked about his daughter. "How is Brooks doing?"

Donovan's sixteen-year-old daughter, Brooks, had given birth to a baby the previous winter, and she had given the baby up for adoption.

"She's getting through day by day, but she hurts, missing the baby. You're the counselor: is there a name for this?"

"Not guessing," Ron said. "What kind of arrangement is the adoption?"

"Double blind. She'll get a letter and a picture every year, but that's all the contact she's allowed to have. She doesn't know where they live, what the family's like, anything. She doesn't even know who the adoptive parents' social worker is."

"Why did you — she, I mean — choose to go that way?"

"She felt strongly it was best for him."

"What's his name?"

"Robert." Donovan's face clouded over for a few seconds.

Ron waited until it had cleared and said, "Can I ask?"

"The adopting parents ..." Donovan's face scrunched up again, cleared again. "They asked that Brooks give a name they could use as a middle name." He blinked several times. "She told them 'Carlton'. I have no idea why."

"How's your wife with all this?"

"Nancy was ... is ... put off. She wanted ... a different ending, one Brooks and I were both against."

Ron nodded slowly. "I see." After a moment he changed the subject. "So where are you working now?"

"You probably already know," Donovan said. "I started two

Mondays ago working for Barringer High School in the central IT facility. After I run their IT for a year, I'm eligible to compete for head of IT for the school system. Ran Androsky is retiring a year from now."

"Congrats. Yeah, after you asked me to be a reference, they came and asked, and I told them about when we worked together before. Speaking of before, was that Nolan McCloskey you were talking to?"

"Yeah. He saw you coming and said bad things about your parents and stalked off."

Ron's lips flinched: Years ago, Donovan wouldn't have hesitated to repeat McCloskey's use of *bastard*. But that was before his teenage daughter had a baby.

Donovan asked "What does he have against you?"

"I was involved in some stuff that went on late last fall with his family — his ex-family, I mean. Did he come to town for the funeral?"

Donovan shook his head. "He was in town to see his kids and heard about the funeral. Is Mason working this case?"

"Yeah, he is."

"You must have seen him since the trial. What has he found out?"

"We talked once, but everything I know has been in the paper," Ron lied.

"Hmm." Donovan looked in Ron's eyes, but knew he wouldn't get anything else out of him.

"I hope you don't mind," Ron said, "but I need to say hello to a couple of other folks."

Donovan nodded and went off to find Nolan McCloskey again.

Ron spotted Henery Guyée. "Eight-ball! We meet again."

"Yes, sir, we do! I was sorry to hear about Mr Book-Man. What do they know 'bout who shot him?"

"You'd have to talk to John Mason about that. He's here someplace."

Mason, after offering personal condolences to the Book-mans, spent his time at the reception chatting to members of the two car clubs that had a presence: The Pantera club and the Lam club.

Quietly, and in the farthest corner of the room from Nathan's parents, he introduced himself as the detective leading the investigation and handed business cards to everyone who came around. The men who weren't wearing excessive gold jewelry had business cards for him; he wrote down the contact info for the rest.

Another of the people who came by was Ruthie Sellers. John told her he worked with Detective Alcalá, and she smiled and said how much she would miss Book and who was the man over there in the black suit?

She could have meant any of half a dozen people, so John asked which one she meant. She pointed, and he said, "That is Ron Penfield. He and I used to work with Nathan years ago."

"He looks like someone who should be married," she said.

"He was. His wife died last year."

Her voice dropped half an octave. "Really. Is he alone now?"

"He has three kids, from college down to middle school. And I think his mother-in-law lives with them at least part time."

John's head turned slowly, and he caught her widened eyes, her straight, turned-up nose in profile, the deep sigh as she looked at his friend.

Across the room, Ron glanced at John and Ruthie, then said hello to someone from Kaiser who would talk to him.

Ruthie said, "When did you say his wife died?"

"A little over a year ago."

"Has he been seeing anyone?"

John smiled. "Not the last I knew."

"All that time without ... a wife."

5:10 p.m.

John was eating a hamburger on the outside patio of a McDonald's as he spoke to Ron, who was in a grocery store, pretending to look at canned vegetables. They were using their prepaid cell phones; both had left their regular phones in their cars. By accident, of course.

John said, "Did Grove and Orozco really give you that hard a time?"

"Yeah," Ron said. "It was bad enough when Bookman's parents started talking about Kaiser at the funeral, but the woman in line behind me interrupted them. Big relief. Yeah, the funeral was an inappropriate place to talk about it."

John swallowed and thought. Ron wasn't being completely coherent, mixing up Tuesday's FBI interview and Wednesday's funeral reception. He asked, "That was bad even for Book's parents. You're certain that was what the Bureau is on about?"

"I can't think of anything else. Surely that's over by now. It's been almost eight years. What could possibly be left to investigate?"

"I think," John said, "they were frustrated with Book's being killed. They're trying to rattle you, I dunno, as a target of opportunity or something."

"Rattle me, shake me."

"Huh?"

"Never mind," Ron said. "There's nothing for them to find."

"If they aren't after you, they could be trying to provoke someone else."

Ron was growing more agitated. "But *eight years*! John, that's not *reasonable*. Not even close."

"Did they say who else they talked to?"

"Not to me. But if they're really cooperating with your investigation, you must know."

John hesitated. "They had a list of people who were at the funeral. They insisted on talking to everyone there who was from Kaiser. Including me."

"How'd that go?"

"They tried good cop/bad cop with me."

"At least you *had* a good cop. With me it was bad cop/worse cop." Ron paused. " *Why is this not over?* "

A lady passing by Ron on the canned vegetable aisle raised her eyebrows but kept going.

John bit his lip to keep from responding.

Ron said, "Who else was on their list?"

"Donovan, Arlie Williams, Eight-ball, McLamb. Oh, and Polino. They didn't ask about anyone who wasn't there."

Ron muttered something under his breath.

"What's that?"

" 'That travesty,' I said. Meaning the funeral."

"You weren't happy with the funeral?"

"No. Were you?"

John thought for a few seconds. "I've been to all kinds of funerals. I've been to Catholic funeral masses, to atheist memorials, to your wife's funeral. I've been to 'celebration services,' whatever the heck that means. I've been to funerals for murder victims, for people who died of cancer, accidents, old age. But this is the first time I've ever thought that the person conducting it — minister, rabbi, close friend, whatever — had no respect whatever for the deceased. It was like a bad evangelistic meeting, and I've been to a couple of those, too."

Ron nodded even though John couldn't see it.

"You get used to it," Ron said. "And then when someone close to you dies, you realize how rotten it is. But that was the worst I've ever heard."

John ate a French fry.

Ron didn't say anything.

"But after eight years," Ron muttered.

"That's enough, Ron." John's patience finally gave out, and he sat up straight in his plastic chair. "Yeah, you're right; the Kaiser shutdown should be over by now. It may even *be* over — they're not telling us what they are investigating. But why might it not be? Why did it happen? It happened because *you* take on things you shouldn't. *You* took on the processor issue back then; you hid Sean McCloskey last fall; you —" He stopped abruptly.

"I what?"

"Never mind."

"*I ... what!?*" Ron was almost shouting.

"That's *enough*."

"You think ... I ... O dear God ..."

John hadn't said it, but Ron worked it out anyhow. He had taken on counseling he should have passed off to someone else. Counseling the girl who would murder his wife.

Ron's hand fell to his side, the call still connected.

"Ron. Ron! *Ron!*" John knew that Ron wasn't listening anymore, so he rang off and called him back.

In the grocery store, Ron's phone, still at his side, rang, but Ron couldn't hear it.

After getting shuffled to voice mail, John hung up and tried again. Voice mail again.

John shrugged. He had to get back to work. He turned off the cell phone and removed the battery, then went back to his car.

Halfway to the station, he had an idea. Using his regular phone, he called the Penfield house. Gloria Heinmeier, Ron's mother-in-law, answered.

John said hello, and asked, "Is Ron home?"

"No, Detective, he isn't. He was going to the grocery store. May I leave a message?"

"I'm worried about him. He and I were supposed to meet, but he never came. Is there a way to check whether he's okay?"

Gloria's eyes narrowed. "He didn't say anything ... I tell you what. I'll call his cell phone, and if he doesn't answer, I'll have one of the children go look for him. May I call back on this number to update you?"

"That would be great, thanks."

They said goodbye, and Gloria called Ron's cell phone, the one she knew about. Straight to voice mail. She rang off, tried again, same result.

She considered for a moment. Ron hadn't mentioned meeting with the detective or anything else; this was to be a quick run to the store. Which, come to think of it, was, for any member of the Penfield family nowadays, unusual. Weird, even.

Gloria ran up the stairs, knocked on Lenna's door, and went in.

139

"Do you have a few minutes dear? I really need you."

"Sure, Grandma."

"Can you drive me to the grocery store? Your father doesn't seem to be coming straight home or answering his phone, and I need something right away."

Lenna nodded and set down her book of poetry.

Gloria returned to the kitchen, and Lenna joined her after a moment. As they went to the car, Gloria said, "I'm so sorry to bother you with this."

"It's okay Grandma, I understand." Gloria's vision problems prevented her from driving.

"If you spot your father while we're on the way to the store, we can turn around and chalk this one up to my impatience." After saying it, Gloria realized this was inconsistent, but Elena didn't seem to notice.

After backing out of the driveway, Lenna said, "Is something going on Grandma?"

Gloria realized hiding things from her granddaughter was a bad idea.

"Did you hear the phone ring a few minutes ago?"

Lenna nodded.

"Detective Mason called. He said your father was supposed to meet him for coffee, but he never arrived. But Ron was only going to the store for a gallon of milk, not to meet anyone, so I got worried. But it's probably nothing."

All the way to the store, they didn't see Ron's car. When they arrived, they found it in the parking lot, so they went inside to look for him.

Inside, Gloria looked around the front of the store for Ron, while Lenna scooted toward the dairy section in a back corner of the supermarket.

Gloria walked along the front, and spotted Ron sitting in the four-table café section.

"Ron, are you all right?"

He stared straight forward, not acknowledging her presence. His hands were both on the tiny café table, one gripping his keys, the other a cell phone.

The store manager, a middle-aged woman, approached. "Ma'am, do you know this man?"

"Yes, he's my son-in-law. Can you tell me what happened?"

"When we found him, he was standing on the canned vegetable aisle holding his cell phone, just standing there with a faraway look on his face. We asked him repeatedly whether there was a problem, and after we asked him several times, he mumbled that he got some bad news."

Lenna walked up, and Gloria sat down opposite Ron.

The manager went on. "I got him to sit down here so he wouldn't creep out the other customers. That was about ten minutes ago."

Gloria listened, but did not look at the manager. "Thank you very much for all your help."

"If there's anything else I can do ..."

"We will let you know. Thank you again."

The manager nodded and backed away to go manage something.

Lenna asked, "Daddy, are you okay?"

Ron didn't respond.

"Do we need to take him to the hospital?"

"Not right now," Gloria said. "But we do need to drive him home."

Gloria tried twice more to get Ron's attention by speaking to him.

When he didn't move, she reached across the table and took both his hands. Suddenly, he focused on their joined hands, then his eyes traced up Gloria's arms, shoulders, neck. When he got to her face, he took on a look of horror and suddenly jerked back, pushing his chair back until it hit the table behind him, nearly tipping it over.

"Gloria! What? ..."

He exhaled and sat breathless like someone plunged into icy water. Forcing himself to breathe, he said, "You ... you must hate me ... hate me ..."

He bit his lip. "Can't blame you."

He shook his head. "Can't."

"Ron," Gloria said, "I don't hate you. I don't know what's going on, but you need to come home with us. With Elena and me."

Suddenly, he couldn't look at Gloria any more. His face scrunched up, and he dug his fists up into his eyes.

None of them moved for a full two minutes.

Finally, Lenna stepped over and put her hands on his.

"Daddy," she whispered. "You need to go home. Come with me; I'll take you."

He looked up at her. For a couple of seconds, he looked as if he would be overcome with joy. But as he focused and realized he was looking at his daughter and not his wife, his joy fell into mourning, and he gasped and sobbed and wept.

Over her shoulder, Lenna said, "Grandma, Ron should be getting out of class about now. Can you call him to come pick you up?"

Gloria said, "Yes, I will. We can work out the extra car later."

Ron responded to Lenna's gentle tug on his hands by getting up and following her to her car.

As they walked away, Lenna stepping lightly and Ron shuffling, Gloria got her cell phone from her purse. As she waited for Ron Jr to answer, she took Ron's keys and the cell phone from the table and dropped them into her purse.

8:54 p.m.

Ruthie gradually climbed out of the hole that Nathan Bookman's murder had thrown her into. She slept, but it was the sleep of drunkenness, not contentment or even mere rest.

But the sleep allowed her to function well enough at work and then get home and drink herself to sleep again. It was the reverse of the coffee cycle some people used to keep themselves awake at work.

She had seen this cycle operate in her father, bad as he was, and she didn't want to repeat it. So, around the fourth night, she had started purposely cutting back on the amount of whiskey, allowing her sleep to become more and more restful.

That brought her to last night: She had only had one short drink and slept almost naturally.

Gerald, the bartender, noticed. "You've been feeling better," he said.

"I don't know whether the wound is healing or just scabbed over," she said. "Did I ever tell you what happened?"

Gerald shook his head *no*.

"I got news a friend was killed. A friend I was close to."

"Boyfriend?"

"Some nights."

Gerald nodded. "How's that bottle of VO holding out?"

"It's gone. I was going to get something else tonight. Johnnie Red, or maybe Jack."

"Okay. Just let me know."

Ruthie worked her tables that night, and the tips rolled in as they seldom had before.

It was Hold 'Em night. She explained to a table of six newbies, who all looked like lawyers pretending to be Texans, "There isn't any gambling for money. You buy in for five dollars and get chips. All the money goes to charity."

"Which charity? MADD?"

They all laughed, and she smiled at the old joke. "It goes to the Lung Association. The owner's mama died of lung cancer."

"And it's just five dollars?"

"That's where it starts. The buy-in doubles every hour, and the winner gets to keep all his chips from game to game."

"So, it's just for braggin' rights?" He affected a Texas drawl, badly.

"Yep. At the end of the night, only one person will ride off with anything to brag about."

That drew snortles all around the table.

After they finished their round of drinks, two of the group decided to buy into the Hold 'Em game, two left for the evening, and the remaining two ordered fresh drinks.

The one with little law-school glasses asked, "Can I buy you a drink?"

"No, thanks," Ruthie said. "I've got to be able to drive home."

He smiled and tilted his head and opened his eyes wide. "Breakfast, perhaps?"

Ruthie drew a breath and closed her eyes. She opened them with a smile and said, "No, thanks" and turned on her heel to pick up drinks for another table.

Gerald noticed her face had acquired a mask of mere duty. "What's the matter?"

"One of the guys at a table just tried to pick me up."

"Which one?"

"Table twenty-four. Glasses"

"Relax. I'll give Mina the table. If he says anything else, I'll tell Danny." Danny was Buckhead's Friendliest Bouncer.

She nodded thanks, and in a minute, she was back to normal.

As Ruthie passed by the Hold 'Em table, she heard one of her lawyers saying, "One more card! Let's take a ride by the river!"

She stopped short and shook her head as if to clear a cobweb from her thoughts. And she remembered. She hoped she hadn't thrown away the detective's phone number.

9:30 p.m.

Jack Robinson handed Whittaker Thomas a mug of decaffeinated coffee. Jeffery Yuen, whose mother was English, set his cup of tea down on the table before they all sat.

These three men, the elders of Trinity Reformed Church, normally met at seven p.m. on Wednesdays, but Whit and his wife had been called to the hospital bedside of a member's granddaughter to referee between the little girl's father and her mother's father, who had fallen out some years before.

"Thanks for meeting so late," Whit said. "Jayne and I had to stand between a pair of hot-blooded Irishmen at the hospital. It took over an hour just to lower the temperature of their discussion."

"No problem for me," Jeff said. "Jack is the one with the early hours."

"I'm fine," Jack replied. "But it would be a favor if we could get started."

Whit nodded and prayed briefly. Then they began discussing the upcoming morning sermons in the current series on the book of Amos; then the evening series that Jack and Jeff were preaching on alternating Sundays.

Finally, they began discussing the needs of the members of the small congregation; each of the three was responsible for understanding how a portion of their members were doing: who had just been laid off from work, who was having problems with children or spouses or in-laws or drinking or gambling.

One of Jeff's responsibilities was the Penfield family. Ron Penfield and Jeff got along well, since they were both computer types. But Jeff was restrained when he said they seemed okay.

Whit asked, "So what has you worried about Ron, Jeff?"

Jeff drew a breath. "I can't really put a finger on it. He still smiles and shakes hands, but the smile never crawls up to his eyes. He knows the routine, but it's a cool routine, not a warm one."

Jack asked, "How long has this been going on?"

"It has been gradual. I didn't notice anything until I came back to town after my business trip and suddenly it was stark." He considered for a moment, eyes half closed. "Thinking back, it may have been before May."

Whit pursed his lips; Jack's eyebrows lowered and he snapped his fingers.

"Of course," Jack said.

"The anniversary of Barb's death," Jeff and Whit said, almost together.

Ron's wife had been killed in April the year before.

"You've known Ron a long time," Whit said to Jack.

"And you were there last year for the family when I was out of town," Jeff added. "Do you have any insight?"

"Not really." Jack shook his head. "He probably still harbors some feelings of guilt over the events that triggered Barbara's death."

"Ron didn't kill his wife," Whit said.

"He knows that," Jack said. "But he can't help what he *feels*. Or thinks he can't. Or thinks he can handle it."

"He got counseling last year," Jeff said. "Maybe he quit too soon. With a delayed reaction like this, he may need to go back."

"Or learn the Gospel all over," Whit said. "Receiving forgiveness can be hard."

Thursday, June 28

Ron sat in darkness. Slivers of light squeezed past the edges of the shades drawn over his office windows. His eyes were closed, trying to prevent any renegade photons from penetrating the gloom permeating every thought.

Kaiser. A hundred families out of work, because Ron knew that with a shortcut — an elaborate, deceptive shortcut that took hours of planning and research and execution — he could make something work. Even if the Army contract didn't allow it.

Sean McCloskey. His sister stressed and his mother physically ill because Ron had to solve the mystery of the senator's murder.

Ronny. *Ron Jr*, he corrected himself. Born when Ron and Barb had only been married for seven months. Barb's college plans put on hold — eventually canceled — because their passion had overruled what they knew was right.

Vicky Winstead.

149

And Barb.

How do you face the responsibility for your own wife's murder? Ron hadn't cut Barb's brake line. But he *had* set the events in motion that led the Winstead girl to seek revenge for being refused. He had taken his counseling of the girl to a level he never should have. Deprived of her father for most of her teenage years, she developed unhealthy affection for Ron, and she wanted to take it further.

Barb died because Ron refused to be unfaithful.

It was his fault.

It was *his* fault.

It was *all* his fault.

All of it was *all* his fault.

That thought replayed in his mind for hours on end.

Lenna or Ed brought him meals on a tray as he brooded in the dark. Sometimes he ate. Sometimes he slept. All the time he inflicted the darkness on himself.

"Slept" — that was way too strong. He closed his eyes and lost consciousness. He had no dreams and got almost no rest.

9:20 a.m.

Ruthie Sellers opened the door for Mark Alcalá. She wore a big, floppy T-shirt, green with yellow lettering that said *CHAPARRAL BASEBALL*; it fell halfway down her thigh, so low Mark couldn't tell whether she was wearing shorts. Barefoot, she came just to the height of his nose. She wore light makeup, except for her lips, where the gloss reflected all the light from the room and may have glowed on their own.

"I'm glad you were able to come by," she said.

"It's not a problem. You mentioned on the phone that you remembered something."

"Mm, hmm. But come on in and sit down. Can I get you some water or lemonade?"

"No, thanks."

Ruthie sat on the border of the center cushion on the end opposite Mark, and turned to face him directly, one knee against the back of the couch with her calf turned across the seat. If she was wearing shorts, they were very short indeed.

"What was it you wanted to add to what you told me?"

"Do you remember how I told you Book and I used to go driving?"

Mark nodded.

"Well . . . there was this one time he decided to drive around the river in east Marietta. Or maybe it was Smyrna. We stopped at a park and tried to go for a walk on the trail by the river, but we turned back after maybe a hundred yards because the mosquitoes were about to carry us off. I wasn't real steady on my feet that night anyway."

"Which car were you driving?"

"We were in the red car that night. The reason I called you back was I remembered we did make one stop at some house around Roswell on the way home. It was in an older neighborhood with little houses."

"Was this recently?"

"It was back in April."

"Did you go in with him?"

"Oh, he didn't go inside. He got an envelope out of the glove box and took it to the door. I heard him talking to someone, then Book was back in the car, and we left."

"Do you have any idea whose house it was?"

"No," she said, leaning toward him, "I'm afraid not."

"Can you describe the person he talked to?"

She shook her head, and some of her hair fell from her shoulder and touched the cushion in front of her. "I couldn't see the front door."

"Did Nathan go inside?"

"I don't *think* so. I only heard the door open once and close once."

She a little closer, and he could detect a breath mint valiantly trying to cover the smell of morning breath.

"Do you think you could find the house or the neighborhood?"

"No, I really don't. Book hadn't had anything to drink yet, but I'd had three or four and nothing to eat and I didn't know that part of town so I couldn't find it if I had to. He told me this guy was ornery, only he said it funny — he might have meant his name was Henri" — her drawl really kicked in as she said *awn-ree* — "and he laughed and said 'Let's go back.'"

"Were you safe to drive later?"

"I stayed all night." She lowered her voice, and when she did, she sounded almost hoarse. "I did that a couple of times."

Mark sat up very straight and pushed back against the armrest.

"So, in April, Nathan Bookman took you for a drive at night in an older neighborhood near the Chattahoochee, and he gave someone an envelope. Was the envelope white? brown? sized for a letter or for a bill? Was anything written on it?"

Ruthie closed her eyes and sat up a little straighter. "It was a Manila envelope that could hold a sheet of paper without folding it. Nothing was written on the front. It was curled up from being in the glove box."

Mark asked, "Can you remember anything else?"

She shook her head and opened her eyes wide, exaggerating their size. "No, I guess not. Like I said, I was under the influence."

She paused, as if trying to remember something.

"The night before he died ... There was a car ..."

She collected her thoughts for a moment.

"I was driving by his house to see whether I could stop by for ... a surprise. And there was a car that looked like it was driving away from his house."

"That could be important," Mark said. "Can you describe it?"

"It was older. A muscle car maybe? It was dark — after midnight — the house lights were all off, so I drove on."

Mark's eyebrows drew together furrowing the skin above his nose. "Did you notice the color? Any characters on the license tag? Any body details?"

Ruthie bit her lip. "No. No, I don't remember any more details."

She slouched a little and suddenly looked exhausted.

Mark relaxed his shoulders and stood up. "I appreciate this additional information. They may be helpful."

Ruthie stood and sighed. "Is that all? I have to go the grocery store and then to work later."

Mark nodded and beat a retreat for the door, words from two different mentors running through his head: *Be the best cop you can be*, and *It'll be your badge on the line*. But he really wanted to ignore them both.

9:30 a.m.

"Grandma, wasn't Clarissa coming over for tea, or whatever ladies have?"

Gloria looked out the kitchen window and across the street to Clarissa Miller's house.

"Yes, Edward, I was expecting her half an hour ago." She half closed her eyes and shook her head slowly. "I hope everything is all right."

"Why don't you go and check on her?"

Gloria let out a long breath and said, "You're right. I think I should."

Gloria slipped through the garage and walked across the street to her friend's front door. At the door, she knocked and called out, "Clarissa, dear, are you home?"

The very weak "Just a minute" Gloria heard furrowed her brow with concern.

When the door finally opened, Clarissa was pale, and her face was taut with pain.

"Sit down!" Gloria ordered.

Clarissa sank into the dining room chair just around from the front door.

"Let me get you some water," Gloria said.

"Please, no," Clarissa whimpered. "I can't hold anything down."

Gloria considered what she was seeing. "Wait right here."

She rushed back across the street, through the kitchen, down the hall into Ron's office. He sat in the dark, leaning back in his leather office chair, eyes closed.

She flipped the light switch.

"Ron, get up. You have to come help."

"No," Ron said flatly, blinking against the sudden invasion of light. "I'm not moving."

"I don't care how you feel. You have to come drive Clarissa to the hospital right away."

"Get Lenna or Ron Jr to do it. Or you drive her."

"Get up and come *now*." Gloria's fist pounded on the desk just as she said *now*. "You know I see badly, and Ron Jr and Elena aren't here. Clarissa can barely walk, and I don't want her to have to wait for an ambulance. Now. Come. *On!*"

Ron sighed and shuffled off to his bedroom for shoes, wallet, and keys.

He's not moving fast, Gloria thought, *but at least he's moving.*

Gloria called to the kitchen, "Edward! Come with us across the street."

Ron backed the minivan out of the driveway and pulled into Clarissa's driveway.

"Come help me get her to the car," Gloria told Ron.

With Gloria holding one arm and Ron holding the other, Clarissa shuffled to the car and got in.

"Where are your house key and your purse, dear?"

"Key rack. Kitchen table."

"Edward, find the house key and bring me Clarissa's purse. After we leave, make sure all the doors are locked. Take the key back home."

Ed nodded and turned toward the kitchen.

"Run!" Gloria said.

Ed sprinted off and returned a moment later with the purse and the keys. As the adults backed out of the driveway, he went back inside to check all the doors.

155

Traffic was light and the traffic signals cooperated, so the trip to the emergency room only took fifteen minutes.

Ron sat with Clarissa in the waiting room as Gloria checked her in. He saw her pain and her tears, and he put her hand around his.

"Squeeze as hard as you want when it hurts," he said.

Clarissa grabbed maniacally and didn't let go.

After a couple of minutes, the triage nurse came over and looked at Clarissa, who was still pale and distraught. The nurse checked Clarissa's pulse rate, temperature, blood pressure, and oxygen level. She asked, "Where does it hurt?"

With her free hand, Clarissa indicated her lower abdomen.

"I'll be right back."

In thirty seconds, the nurse returned with a wheelchair. She and Ron helped Clarissa into the chair, and Gloria followed as the nurse wheeled her to an examination room.

Ron sat and flexed his hand to recover some circulation.

Ron waited in the emergency waiting room. After time that seemed interminable, Gloria came out and fetched him, explaining that Clarissa was on her way to an emergency appendectomy.

When Ron said he wanted to return home, Gloria said, "We will do no such thing! We'll go wait in the surgery waiting room, and we'll stay until Clarissa is safe and out of surgery."

"Does she not have any family? Locally, I mean?" Ron noticed that Gloria was holding a cell phone in her hand that was not her own. As they continued snaking through the endless hallways, he asked, "Is that Clarissa's phone?"

"Locally, no. And yes, this is her phone. While we were

waiting for the surgeon, Clarissa gave it to me and asked me to call her mother."

"And?"

The pair reached the waiting area and found adjacent seats. They sat, and Gloria answered.

"And her mother lives about three hours away. She won't be able to come up until tomorrow."

Ron was surprised. "For her own daughter?"

"She has to ... regain her ..."

After a pause, Ron whispered, "Sobriety?"

Gloria nodded.

"Well," Ron said, "at least she'll be able to stay at Clarissa's. I wonder whether she will be able to care for her daughter when she gets here."

"If she can't, we may end up doing for her for a few weeks. I suppose I will need to cancel plans."

"We can wait to see what her mother can do."

"I suppose so," Gloria said.

After a wait of a couple of hours, Gloria was called to consult with the surgeon, and Ron went along as well.

The surgeon, who looked about the right age for the braces fitted on his teeth, told them, "Ms Miller's appendix ruptured, and spilled some fluid into her abdominal cavity. We will have to keep her in isolation for a couple of days to lower the risk of infection."

Gloria asked, "Will she be able to see visitors?"

"Yes, but they'll have to put on protective clothing to go into her room."

As he was speaking, Ron thought and remembered. "She has been having occasional abdominal pain. Could her appendix have been the cause of it?"

The surgeon answered in the affirmative, and then Gloria and Ron thanked him and went back to the waiting area.

When Gloria sat, Ron remained standing and asked, "Can I get you tea or something. Perhaps a snack or even a meal? The hospital café is just around the corner."

"A sandwich would be good," Gloria said. "It doesn't matter much what kind. And a cup of tea with it would be just the thing."

"Just sugar, yes?"

Gloria nodded, and Ron rounded the corner in search of food.

When he returned with food for both of them, Gloria thanked him.

As they ate, Ron said, "It's too bad we won't be able to see Clarissa while she's in isolation."

"You won't but I will," Gloria said. "Just before the surgery, she signed a directive that said I am to be treated as family. Which is good, because it will allow me to assess her mother's fitness to take care of her."

7:00 p.m.

Lenna was loading the dishwasher when the doorbell rang, so she called out to her brother to see who it was.

"Hi, Pastor," Ed said.

"Hi, Ed. May I go see your dad?" Whitaker Thomas asked.

"Sure."

Whit stepped into the foyer and asked, "So how do you read this? How he's doing, I mean?"

Ed's lips trembled. "I don't know what to think. I mean,

some people like to be alone, but for Dad to get this extreme about it is too much. He had to study alone when he was in school a few years ago, but it was never like this. He just sits there in the dark."

"Does he eat meals, drink water?"

"Yes, sir. Lenna and I take turns taking him meals. He usually eats a few bites, but sometimes he just skips a meal, and we pick up the tray when we take him the next one."

"He doesn't eat with everyone else, then?"

Ed shook his head. "And he only eats a little, even when we take him one of his favorites."

Whit nodded.

"What about how he acts when you do go in there? What does he do?"

"Sometimes he'll say, 'Thanks,' but most of the time he just grunts."

"Have you tried asking him to help you with something?"

"With school out, we don't need homework help. And when a light bulb went out and we didn't have the right kind, he just gave me his credit card and told me to ride my bike to the convenience store. Not a hardware store or anything."

"It's not like him to waste the extra money like that."

"I know," Ed said. "It's like he's someone totally different."

Whit ventured into Ron's office. A few minutes later, after abusive words had cascaded over him from behind the desk, he left.

8:00 p.m.

John had put it off long enough: he had sent a text message to Lilia, asking if they could talk at eight o'clock.

Mason left the office a few minutes early to try to get his mind into a settled frame before calling, but as eight o'clock approached, his agitation only grew. He came within a hair's breadth of texting Lilia to cancel, but his promise to his current wife overrode his desire to avoid his previous wife.

Calling her cell phone, as she had requested, after brief hellos and a quick update about their daughter (no different from all previous updates), Mason said, "I told you to leave Ann alone. Why did you call her? What changed that made you need to interrupt our life?"

Lilia's voice, low-pitched and silky, her Greek accent still coloring her pronunciation, asked, "Is it so unreasonable to ask a father to take an interest, an *active* interest in his daughter? That is all I am asking, John. For you to be a father. To be *Adena's* father."

"So, are we talking about weekends? overnights? what?"

"It is not about quantity, like paying at the grocery store and expecting groceries. It is not transactional. It is about *being*, not *doing*."

When John didn't respond after a few seconds, Lilia went on: "She needs a father so she knows what to expect from a boy, and what the limits are."

"Does she really? She's atypical. Not to put too fine a point on it, but will anyone be interested in her?"

That hung in the air for a full minute. When Lilia responded, it was in a tone John knew far too well as fuming anger.

"John, she is not unpretty. Maybe she has not discovered it yet, and maybe her life will be unlike others, but you know some boys will chase down anything in a skirt and take pride in attaining the unattainable, or rare, for the bragging rights if nothing else."

He knew Lilia was speaking from her own experience. When she had come to the U.S. for college, frat boys had referred to her as the "Greek goddess" and made her the constant target of their libido.

"Can't your boyfriend teach her these things? You are fairly picky about men. You wouldn't be seeing anyone who's not trustworthy."

"There is no one now, John."

"She requires constant care, and you have no one to help. I'm your last hope, huh?"

"You act like she is an invalid. She is not. She goes to school, and she requires extra attention, yes. And she may never live totally on her own. But she is near genius. And she remembers everything."

"Do you think . . . she would want to see me? Or does she remember how I . . . abandoned her? And you?"

"I do not know whether she would think of it. But if I ask her, she will see you because she trusts me."

After a pause, John said, "I'll start seeing Adena when I can. But I can't promise a regular schedule. Criminals don't have fixed schedules."

"When do you think you can see her?"

"It won't be this weekend, and probably not next week. I'm in a major investigation, a murder, and I'm working long hours."

"All right," Lilia said. "There has to be some accommodation to both our lives — to *all* our lives."

8:15 p.m.

Wal-Marts permeate the south, almost to the same degree of saturation as churches. That's why Mason had been able to visit three different stores without ever going more than ten miles from his house. At each one, he bought a cell phone and prepaid fifty dollars for voice, text and MMS on each. With cash.

In each phone, he had entered the numbers for his own prepaid phone and for two of the others into each phone's address book, and he set up an email account on each phone. Finally, he removed the batteries and put each phone and its battery in a Zip-Lock bag in his trunk.

Now he waited in the parking lot of a small neighborhood's community swimming pool, leaned against the trunk of his car.

A mom who was leaving the pool with two small children in tow appeared abruptly and asked him what he was doing there. Mason showed her his badge and explained that he was meeting one of the subdivision's residents. As the woman and her kids exited the parking lot on foot, she pointedly glanced back from the corner of her eye at him.

A low-pitched rumble gradually intruded itself on Mason's hearing. He smiled as a mid-seventies Duster drove in, royal blue with a wide white stripe down the center of the hood; the stripe was the same width as the air scoop.

When the engine cut off, he smiled. "Eight-ball! What a

great car!"

"Thanks, Mr Mason. It's good to see you. Did you know I saw Mr Penfield a few days ago?"

"Ron told me about that. You were in the ... hardware store?"

Guyée nodded his bald head. "Why are we here?"

"We have one more person on the way," Mason said. "And call me John."

"I'll try to remember."

A maroon Volvo, about the same age as Eight-Ball's Duster but much quieter, rolled in and parked between the Duster and Mason's Infinity.

Carlton Donovan shook hands with both of the others.

Mason asked, "Is that the same car? Last time I saw it, it was almost as loud as Eight-ball's."

Carlton smiled. "Once I got a regular job, I was able to get some work done on it. It was running like a champ, even when it needed a muffler. So, what's this about?"

"Okay," Mason said, "here's the deal. We've all been interviewed by the FBI since Bookman died. We know he was murdered, but the feds are holding their cards close to the chest about why they are interested. I think it's related to Kaiser Transceivers. As people with different perspectives, I want us to keep an eye out for what they're doing, and for any sightings of ex-Kaiser employees."

Eight-ball asked, "So we're spying on people?"

Mason shook his head. "No, nothing like that."

Carlton said, "A lot of those folks still live around here. Robinson, for instance. And Getty and Sebastian."

"And a lot more," Mason agreed. "I'm not sure how to say this. If you see someone from Kaiser you haven't seen in a long

163

time, or if you see someone in the wrong place at the wrong time — I'm not even sure what I mean — If you see someone you knew at Kaiser out and about — in the grocery store or the hardware store or out in traffic — anywhere, really — just make a mental note and tell the other two."

"Do we call you when we see someone?" Eight-ball asked. "Should I write down your number?"

"Not exactly." Mason opened the trunk of his car and gave them both one of the bags of cell phone. Eight-ball's was marked "U"; Donovan's was marked "O".

"There's one more phone," Donovan said. "Who's it for?"

"I'm thinking about pulling one more person into this; I'll let you know who if I do."

Eight-ball nodded.

Donovan asked, "How about Ron Penfield?"

Mason blinked a couple of times. "I can't explain why, but Ron can't help us right now. If he comes into it later, I'll let you know."

Then he explained about the phones, why the batteries were out, and asked that they not use the phones when their other phones were around.

"Whatever you see, text or email both of the other phones, or leave me a voice message. I'll turn on my phone once a day to pick everything up. I will also send you anything significant I see."

Eight-ball said, "What I don't understand is *why?* Are we trying to stop the FBI?"

"No. We're being ... extra eyes and ears for them. If we don't find anything, then they won't know about us. If we do, we will explain the whole thing."

Donovan asked, "Is this illegal? Or unethical, maybe? Privacy and all that."

"No, but I'm glad you asked. We are citizens sharing with our friends observations of people in public *only*. There is no rights violation, and everything we tell each other will be public. Even though we keep it private. We are *coordinating* observations."

After both of the others shook Mason's hand and the detective left, Donovan said to Eight-ball, "I'm kind of surprised you are still shaving your head."

" 'There's many a man has more hair than wit.' I figure without hair, I can keep the ratio favorable."

"Wait," Carlton Donovan said, "that sounds familiar."

"*The Comedy of Errors*," Eight-ball said.

"Is that really why you shave your head?"

Eight-ball snickered. "Not really. I just wanted to get rid of the heat. I work outside enough that it makes sense."

"Not many maintenance men go around quoting Shakespeare. You must read a lot."

"Not as much as when I was in college."

"You've been to college?"

"I'm six hours short of a BA in English."

"Really? Where?"

"Tulane."

"Got any more good quotes?"

" 'False face must hide what the false heart doth know.' "

"*Julius Caesar?*"

Eight-ball shook his head. "The Scottish Play."

Carlton blinked. "Oh, *Macbeth*."

Donovan considered this new side of Eight-ball. "So, why'd you work as a janitor? And now as a maintenance man?"

"When he was sober and not trying to rob people sitting in

the pews, my daddy used to say, 'Henery True — he always used my middle name — somebody got to dig ditches.' Now think about Detective Mason: When he was designing circuits at Kaiser, he was there all kinds of crazy hours. And so were the people who were working for him. Same thing with Mr Penfield when he was at Kaiser making software. And you, yourself, you worked forty a week, but you were on call around the clock. Me? After I do my job, I go home. I may not have as many toys, or eat at restaurants as nice, but when I go home, I can be at home. I didn't have to take my work home with me, and I still don't."

Donovan nodded. "And in my new job, it's still about the same and it won't get any better: I work for the school system keeping the network up and managing servers. Seems like my destiny."

Eight-ball snorted lightly. "So how is your family? How is Little Miss Brooks?"

Donovan's mouth twisted and his eyebrows lowered, forming a crease between them.

"Brooks," he said finally, "has had to grow up a lot in a hurry in the last year. More than she should have had to."

Donovan didn't say any more for a minute.

Eight-ball waited.

Finally, Donovan's face relaxed, and he asked, "So where'd you get the Duster? They've got to be pretty rare anymore."

Eight-ball grinned and said, "Found it at an estate sale. An old geezer had it, and when he died, his kids didn't have any use for it. It hadn't been started in about a decade, so I had to tow it to a place I could work on it. Now ... now she purrs like a kitten."

They went on talking about cars for a few minutes, both

reminiscing about their old cars. They both remembered Nathan Bookman's cars and grinned about them.

Eventually, Donovan said, "I've got to get home. It's good to see you."

Eight-ball reciprocated and climbed into the Duster to head out. Carlton did the same in the Volvo.

When Eight-ball started his car and drove out, Donovan listened for a few seconds and thought, *If that's what 'purrs like a kitten' sounds like, I'd hate to hear the lion roar.*

9:22 p.m.

At home that night, Mason was discussing the conspiracy with his Ann. They were taking a walk in their neighborhood; both had left their phones inside the house. It was a different kind of risk for the two of them: If John missed an official police call, he risked being chewed out; Ann's business was high-end residential real estate, and a missed call, even that late at night, could mean a missed business opportunity in the tens or hundreds of thousands of dollars.

John told Ann who he had chosen to help with noticing things as they went on.

"What are you not telling them, John?"

He waved at a neighbor. "I'm not telling them why I picked them in particular."

Ann waved at a neighbor who was spreading mulch in his flowerbeds as darkness descended, and she waited.

"I wanted them because, for different reasons, they both went everywhere at Kaiser. Between them, they knew everyone who worked there. They *do* know it's related to Nathan

167

Bookman's murder. Seeing people around might jog a memory of a hushed meeting or something out of place. Or ... I don't know."

"So, you're shooting in the dark."

"From a Sopwith Camel, and without tracers."

"And you don't even know who the Red Baron is."

"Or what part of the sky he's in."

"Or how far is too far to go with an analogy."

They smirked at each other for a moment.

"Can they both be trusted?"

John thought for a minute.

"Yeah. Donovan had the highest clearance. He had to be able to work on anyone's computer. And that was a big deal."

"And the janitor?"

"He didn't have any classified access. Heck, he had to be escorted when he was emptying trash cans in classified areas. But he knew everyone, and I believe he knows how to keep his mouth shut when he needs to."

As they reached their own front door, John said, "I finally talked to Lilia this evening."

"And?"

"And she understands my times to see Adena have to be flexible."

Ann nodded and he unlocked the door.

11:32 p.m.

Ruthie wondered what had made the cute detective ask her for a date. She was surprised when he called right before she went to work. That morning, when he came to her apartment, she was hung over, and he must have realized it.

But she smiled to herself now. *It wasn't me he was rejecting, it was the whiskey.* Her heart and her face warmed with the thought, *He likes me, but he wants me to be fully conscious, fully aware when we're together. To be* present, *not stupefied and oblivious.*

When he called, he asked what time she got off work. She said eleven thirty and why did he want to know?

"I want to buy you a late dinner," he had said.

"Okay, where?"

He gave her the address of a place on the east side of downtown Atlanta.

"Are they really open that late?"

"It's open all night," he said, "and they have unbelievable omelets."

So here she was, driving to meet him, and she was glad she got off a few minutes early.

As she turned off Ponce de Leon the neighborhood wasn't looking so good. There were still a few stores, and a convenience store that hadn't closed yet. Two more blocks and turn right, then a block down on the left, his instructions said.

She drove to the address and stopped. There were three abandoned storefronts and a small, neighborhood grocer, which was closed. A couple of guys hung out in front. Trees blocked all the streetlights except the one directly in front of the grocery.

One of the men there, short, but powerfully built, walked over to her car. Her stomach tightened up inside, but her windows were closed, her doors locked, and the car was still in drive. So, she waited.

The man called out so he could be heard through the window, "Are you Miss Ruth?"

She nodded.

"I'm a friend of Mark's," he said. His accent was a little funny. "He said he was wrong about the café being open, but would you go to this address?" He held up a piece of notepaper; she could see writing on it.

She chewed on the inside of her cheek for a moment, then lowered her window an inch. The man slipped the paper to her and walked away. She relaxed as she put the window back up, then drove back to the main drag and found a lighted parking lot where she could check the note.

It gave an address in Decatur, an easy drive down Ponce de Leon. Ruthie got her GPS out of the glove compartment, turned it on, and entered the address from the note. While waiting for it to catch up to her current location, she drove east, not in any real hurry.

A few blocks short of downtown Decatur, she followed the instructions of the annoying, tireless voice through a couple of turns, then stopped when she heard "You have arrived."

Not a restaurant. Not a storefront. Just a house. Run down. In a rotten neighborhood. A badly lit street where most of the light from streetlights was blocked by enormous trees. Too many places to be surprised from without any warning. Dangerous.

She started to drive away when she spotted Mark standing in the cone of light from the only streetlight that wasn't blocked.

Ruthie parked a few yards away from him and got out of her car. She smiled as she walked toward Mark but stopped about six feet away. There was something wrong — he wasn't smiling; he was slouched, not standing straight.

He looked into her eyes and said, "I'm really sorry."

To one side Ruthie saw something flash and heard it pop, and she felt a sting in her chest.

The small bullet ignored the soft tissue of her breast, keeping its shape. When it nicked a rib, it began to tumble and mushroom, and by the time it got to her heart, its cross section was more than tripled.

She gasped and fell to her knees and then over to one side on the sidewalk, and bled out, shocked silent from the partnership of lead and betrayal. Her last thought was, *Why is someone pointing a white stick at me?*

From the shadows, a voice. "What's bothering you, Marco?"

Alcalá blinked back tears and caught a breath. "She didn't *do* anything," he said. "The night she went to your house with Bookman she was too drunk to remember where she was. Heck, she barely remembered being *with* Bookman. You could have let her go."

"And she saw my car leaving his house," the Handler said. "Look, Marco, you just can't afford to fall in love in this business. She was a danger to me, to the operation, to you. You've got to let go of her. And you can't be sorry I had to do this."

Alcalá blinked and nodded, got in his car and drove west, then north into Buckhead. He found a western bar, the Chaps & Spurs, the bar Ruthie worked in — *used to* work in — and went in and drank. His first two drinks were White Russians, then he finished off the night drinking vodka neat until the last call. After they locked the door behind him, he walked to a motel and checked himself in.

When he woke to his cell phone alarm at seven a.m., he

called the station and left word for Mason that he would be in around noon, then set his alarm for ten forty-five and went back to sleep.

Friday, June 29

Jack Robinson watched a truck unload a pallet of bricks at a job site. His apprentice supervisor, Raúl, spotted for the lift operator as he deposited the pallet in the place they had picked out and leveled a couple of days before.

Together they uncovered the bricks and performed the delivery inspection. Jack's right arm was in a sling, so Raúl signed for the delivery, and the truck was on its way.

Jack's cell phone rang and vibrated on his belt, and he fumbled with it in his left hand until he could get a look at the display. He smiled when he saw the number on his caller ID and pressed the button to answer.

"Hi, there, Ron. How are you?"

"Mr Robinson it's not my dad, it's Lenna."

Jack paused for a second. Lenna would only call him because he and Ron were friends, and because Jack was an elder at their church, Trinity Reformed. "Is everything okay?"

Lenna took a turn pausing. "No, sir. No, sir, it isn't. It isn't okay at all."

"What's wrong?"

"Daddy ... he's not all right. He ... something happened we don't understand, and Daddy won't come out of his office and he barely eats or sleeps."

Jack thought back to what Whit Thomas had told him about his visit to Ron. "Tell me what happened in order. Then we'll try to figure out what it is."

"The last few weeks, since the anniversary ..."

"Since the anniversary of your mom's death, right?"

"Yes, sir. Since then, Daddy has been more and more agitated and irritable. It started with little things — a word snapped here and there, a grunt of impatience."

After a brief pause she went on. "Last week at dinner — I think it was Wednesday — he blew up at everyone. He made fun of Ron. He apologized the next day to everyone."

Jack asked, "He apologized individually or to everyone at once?"

"He came to us individually. But Wednesday afternoon — two days ago, I mean —, he went for milk to the grocery store. While he was gone, Grandma got a phone call from Mr Mason."

"The detective?"

"Yes, sir." Lenna explained how they found Ron in the store.

"Did you notice anything out of place? Anything ... unusual?"

"When store manager found Daddy, he was holding a cell phone. The phone was on the table in the café when we got there, but it's not Daddy's regular phone."

Jack's eyebrows fell as he thought for a moment. "That

174

could mean anything," he murmured. *Including what it usually means*, he thought. "Wait," he said. "You said he was talking to Detective Mason. Was this using the new phone?"

"Yes, sir. But since we found him there, he has shut down. Even more than he was since it all started."

"Jeff Yuen mentioned something about him at the last elders' meeting. Has it been like it was before, years ago? You used to call it his 'dark time.'"

"Yes, sir, it's like that, but worse. Back then he would eat dinner with us, even if he never said anything. He helped take a neighbor to the hospital, but now he won't leave his office for anything."

"Tell you what," he said after a moment. "Would it be okay if I came by in a little while? My crew is just starting a job, and after they get going, I'll head over."

"Please do. Is there anything I can do in the meantime?"

"When I'm a few minutes away, I'll call. It would be a favor if you start a pot of coffee when I call. Do you have a cell phone?"

"Yes, sir. Why?"

"Text the number to me, and I'll call you on that number. You can have the phone on vibrate so your dad won't hear it ring and wonder what's going on. Is anyone else home?"

"Ed is here, but he's still in bed. Ron Jr drove Grandma to a doctor appointment."

"Okay. Make sure Ed is up by the time I get there."

They rang off, and Jack gave the crew their starting instructions.

"Look," he said to Raúl, "I've got to go see someone for a while. I'll be gone most of the morning." He reminded Raúl who on the crew were new and would need extra supervision.

Raúl managed to keep from rolling his eyes.

Jack saw his effort and said, "I know you know all this, but it's my job to tell you the stuff you already know. Welcome to the Department of Redundancy Department welcomes you."

Raúl laughed at the symmetry of the old joke.

After forty-five minutes of watching Raúl supervise the crew, Jack nodded and said, "I'm headed out now. If I'm not going to be back by lunchtime, I'll call you."

Raúl nodded and walked around the corner of the house.

Once Jack was on the way, he called his wife, Robin, to tell her where he was going to be, then he pulled off in a parking lot to send a group message to Whit Thomas and Jerry Yuen.

His last call was to Lenna Penfield, to tell her to start the coffee.

As he drove, Jack reflected on what Lenna had told him. From Lenna's description, this was worse than when Ron realized how much all the people laid off at Kaiser had been hurt.

Jack drove toward the Penfields' neighborhood concentrating on his friend rather than on driving. He stopped his truck at a red light, then went on into the intersection, unconsciously thinking of it as a four-way stop sign. But the light hadn't changed, and a small pickup truck, half the size of Jack's, hit the brakes, but was still going about forty-five when it hit his driver's door. Despite seat belt and air bags, Jack was knocked unconscious.

He came to as EMTs cut him out of his seat belt and checked for broken bones and spinal injury before removing him. His neck was immobilized by a brace. When they were satisfied that he could be moved, they pulled him out the passenger-side door (the driver's door was a lost cause) and onto a gurney.

"I've got ..." he tried to start as they strapped him down.

"Don't try to talk," an EMT said as they slid him into the ambulance.

"But Ron ..."

"Whoever Ron is will have to wait," as the oxygen mask went over his face.

"Wife. Robin. Cell phone."

"Yes sir, we'll make sure she's called," as the doors slammed shut.

After that, Jack didn't remember anything.

9:00 a.m.

The MP inspected the maintenance man's ladder, then his box of batteries. She had already checked his credentials (driver's license, job order, and a call to the maintenance contractor's office confirming the name and general description). In all, it took fully half an hour to get through all the hoops.

"You gotta be careful, huh?" Eight-ball asked.

"Yes, we do, Mr Guyée," Corporal Dana Engel said. "I appreciate your patience while we go through all this. When we were trying to do this yesterday, the guy they sent out got huffy about his time being wasted. His attitude was so bad, the Lieutenant sent him away and called your boss and told him to send someone else."

"Yeah, Schimmel, he don't like to wait. Me, I used to work for a defense contractor, so I know these things take time. And call me Eight-ball if you don't mind. Save *mister* for somebody in a suit."

Because Eight-ball's truck carried the forty-foot ladder he

177

was going to need, they both climbed into it for the drive to the warehouse.

"You're not from Georgia," Engel said.

"No, ma'am. I'm from N'w Orleans." He exaggerated the accent a little. "But I've been here for ten years or so."

"So, what do you think of the Saints this year?"

"I don't really follow football, but my cousin is a fiend for it, and he says their chances are about even. Where are you from, Corp'l? You're not from Georgia either."

"I'm from Boise, Idaho."

"How you like the summers here?"

"This is my first summer in the south. I don't think I like it."

"Now what you ought to do," Eight-ball said, "is to like it now and wait till August to be unhappy. That's when the heat and the humidity flip a coin every day to see which one will be higher."

Engel smiled at that.

"You got a pretty smile Corporal. I bet you got no problems getting dates."

"Plenty of guys ask, but not the kind I'm interested in."

Eight-ball nodded. "It's okay. Just do the world a favor and don't wait till you find someone perfect. There ain't none."

"I'll remember that. And you can call me Dana. Which defense company did you work for?"

Eight-ball turned left into the entrance to the warehouse complex. The sign read *Fifth Street Magazine*. "I worked for Kaiser Transceivers up until they shut down."

"Really?" Engel said. "One section of the warehouse has boxes labeled Kaiser Transceivers."

"I guess that's why this place is so secure. But after so

many years since the shutdown, why are these boxes still here? I figured they would have been disposed of by now."

Eight-ball stopped at the gate and pressed the button on the intercom.

"Yes?" came the tinny voice.

The MP leaned across to speak into the intercom. "This is Corporal Engel. I'm here with the maintenance man to repair the smoke alarms."

"Glad you're here. These things are driving me crazy." The gates on the dual fence began to open in opposite directions. "Drive up to the office. First building on the right."

As they walked to the office after exiting the truck, Engel said, "It's probably still here because of budget rerouting. After nine-eleven it was cheaper to store it for the short term, so the 'short term' became very nearly permanent."

At the office, they showed their credentials and signed the entry log as the smoke detector beeped. Engel asked the young woman working in the office, "Why is this place called a 'Magazine'?"

"No idea," the young woman replied from behind huge eyeglasses. She implied, *And I don't care, either* as the smoke detector beeped. Again.

Both women were surprised when Eight-ball said, "It's because one of the French words for warehouse is *magasin*."

"I guess that makes sense," Engel said.

They thanked the receptionist and stepped across the wide, concrete driveway to the large double doors of the warehouse entrance.

"How we goin' to do this?" Eight-ball asked.

"We'll go inside so you can get a feel for the place, then we'll come back for your tools and supplies. While we're inside, the door will be locked behind us. You'll be accompanied at all times."

"Just like when I was a janitor at Kaiser, and I had to go into the secure areas."

Engel held the switch and light from mercury vapor bulbs held in huge, overhead fixtures grew over a couple of minutes, flooding the warehouse.

Shelves ran to thirty feet high and sixty feet long. Four ranks of shelves made up each block, and there were nine blocks, grouped in a three-by-three grid. On the ceiling, smoke detectors were placed every thirty feet in both the length and breadth of the room, starting about fifteen feet from each wall.

Eight-ball looked up and all around, and he nodded.

"My requisition says I'm supposed to replace all the batteries in the detectors, so we're going to be here for a while."

"My orders said the same thing," Engel confirmed.

They went back out the door, and Eight-ball got the ladder.

Engel propped both doors open, then followed Eight-ball with one of the boxes of batteries. After he fetched the other box, she locked the door behind them.

They worked their way up and down the rows of shelves. Each time the ladder was positioned, Eight-ball would pocket a battery and make the climb to the ceiling, replace the battery in the smoke detector, and climb back down.

They stopped about once every hour for a brief break. During the first break, Eight-ball said, "Just lookin' around, I see four cameras looking down the main aisles. Have you seen anything else, Dana?"

"Yeah, there are six cameras in here, and they're monitored in the office where we checked in. You'll see the others as you keep working. They also get a signal from all the smoke detectors, and one or two of those have been beeping every couple of minutes in the office for the last two days because of the low battery."

"It's hard to believe that's all the cameras there are."

"There are alarms on the doors and the skylights, too. But that's all there is in here." Engel knew better, but her training told her to confirm only the obvious and volunteer nothing. If Guyée didn't know about the spot checks, it wouldn't hurt anything.

During their second break, Eight-ball said, "I saw the Kaiser boxes. Me and a couple of others actually carried them in here ourselves."

"Really? I guess that brought back old times."

"It sure did."

Engel asked, "After the shutdown, were the people able to get work? You and the others who helped you, I mean?"

"Yeah," Eight-ball answered, "of the three of us, one went off and became a policeman. He's a detective now. The other fella works in computers for the school system."

"What about everyone else?"

"Mos' got other work. A few had a hard time, but somebody set up a fund to help folks who needed it."

He thought for a minute. "I tell you what, Corp'l Dana, this is going to go on into the afternoon. How about I buy us some lunch and we finish after that?"

They stopped for half an hour and drove out for fast food. When they returned, Engel went into the office while Eight-ball leaned against the outside wall of the office.

When Engel emerged, she said, "Looks like we've solved the alarm problem. Let's finish up and go home."

"That's a winner," Eight-ball said.

181

9:00 a.m.

Grove and Orozco, the FBI agents, had called a dozen names on their list, choosing for this part of the exercise the people who appeared to be members of Bookman's two car clubs.

They got appointments with seven; four didn't answer their phones; one told them they didn't need an appointment if they called a few minutes ahead.

The interviewees fell into three groups: professionals (doctors, lawyers, the head of a corporate accounting department); trust fund kids (most in their thirties, one in his fifties); executives for large companies.

On the way to their first appointment, around the time Eight-ball and Engel were arriving at the warehouse, Grove got a phone call. After arguing with his wife, he rang off.

"Sorry you had to hear that," he said to Orozco.

"It's not a problem for me," Orozco said. "It's tough being married to a cop. If you need to talk, just let me know."

"Thanks."

Orozco dodged a stupid driver and muttered something in Spanish Grove couldn't understand.

Grove leafed through the notebook containing the preliminary backgrounds on the people they were interviewing that day.

Though his mind registered individual words, he paid no attention to what he saw. After a couple of silent, distracted minutes, he said, "It's just, well, Sandra wants a bigger car, and we can't afford it right now because we bought a house that was too big, and the market is weakening in our area."

Orozco, five years Grove's senior, said, "Rob, listen. The

house you can get out of as long as there's not a big crash. The car you can buy. It's none of my business, but if she's yelling that much, the house and the car are just symptoms. Before you came to the Bureau, what did you do?"

"I got a bachelor's in architecture."

They pulled into the parking lot adjacent to their destination but postponed the rest of the conversation because they barely had time to make it to the interview.

Of the executives, the interview with Adrian Brinson was typical. After introductions and the offer and refusal of coffee, Brinson asked, "What can I help you with?"

"We're cooperating with the Bristow police," Grove said, "in the investigation into Nathan Bookman's death."

"Yes, the paper said the police were investigating his murder, though not many details have been released. How did he die?"

"He was shot," Orozco said.

"Suicide?"

"The evidence says no."

Brinson nodded. "Cautious commitment. Or you're holding cards you aren't sure of, and you don't want to tell me."

Grove smiled in recognition. "You've done interviews before."

"I hire the entry-level account executives. Many are too eager to be sure of facts they don't have. Your restraint would make you a likely hire."

Orozco said, "Thanks. But we don't mean to take up any more of your time than is needed. What can you tell us about Nathan Bookman? For instance, what did you call him? Nathan? Nate?"

"It was always 'Bookman.' I asked him once what he did

for a living, and he said he was a consultant. Of course, by itself that carries no information. I was looking for someone to iron out a problem we had, and he said his field was statistical mathematics. That was a more esoteric specialty than we needed at the time, so I didn't pursue hiring him."

"Can you tell me anything about his personal life? Did he ever bring anyone with him to the club meetings?"

"Once he brought a woman. She was younger than he was, in her early- to mid-twenties; had long brown hair and was built 'like a Mexican road.'"

Orozco said "What?", but Grove laughed as he recognized the reference.

"Erle Stanley Gardner," Grove said. " 'Treacherous and full of curves.'"

Brinson nodded.

"Was she Mexican?" Orozco asked.

"No, she was Anglo, from the Southwest, I think," Brinson said. "And more curves than danger."

"How many times was she at your meetings?"

"Just once. She accidentally put scratch in the passenger door of someone's Ferrari. Bookman paid for the repair without blinking, but she never came back to the meetings."

"Besides the company of this woman, was there anything else?"

"Bookman was a fiend for sports statistics. People would ask him about baseball picks, and he was right way more than half the time on the unlikely games. But he never gave anyone more than two games a week."

"Is it possible he made his living that way?"

"He could have, if his betting was cold-hearted."

"Meaning ... ?"

"Meaning if he stayed uninvolved emotionally."

"Did he ever get any phone calls when you were in a meeting?"

"He got one last fall. It was in the middle of a talk some factory rep was giving. The Alfa Romeo rep, I think."

"Alfas aren't sold in the US," Orozco said. "Why was he talking to you?"

"About a year ago, they announced they were returning to the US market, but it hasn't happened yet. I think he said next year."

"About the phone call: Do you remember anything about it?"

"I don't recall any of the words, but I have the impression that someone wanted an appointment."

"Do you know the date?"

Brinson turned to his computer and brought up the calendar. "We met on ..." He paged back through the months. "It was October second."

Grove made a note of the date. Both agents thanked Brinson and left.

Back in the car, Orozco asked, "Where is your house?"

"South of Stafford, in the woods."

"Close to Quantico then."

Grove nodded.

"Look, we've all got priorities, and we all have to work out our families our own way. My wife and I, if we see each other too often we both get nervous."

"What are you saying?"

"I'm saying that there's a lot of work for analysts at Quantico, and your architecture background might help you see things somebody else might miss."

Grove shook his head.

Orozco said, "I'm not saying any more. But you've got career options in the Bureau, or maybe in Langley or Fort Meade."

"I'm not really a signals type," Grove said. *But,* he thought, *Langley might not be too bad. And it would give us an excuse to get out from under the house.*

Later that morning, Grove and Orozco interviewed a couple of young men who were living off inheritance. One was Craig Dorman, whom they found just coming off the court at his tennis club.

At the juice bar (certified organic) Dorman offered the agents a drink. Grove said no thanks; Orozco accepted a Pineapple-Guava.

"So, what do you want, gentlemen?"

Grove explained the situation and asked how well Dorman knew Nathan Bookman.

"Bookman? I don't know ... he helped me buy my DeTomaso. I offered him a fee — half of what he saved me — but he said he didn't want anything."

Orozco asked, "How did he help?"

"When I was looking for a car, I had three prospects, and he helped me sort out which one was best. I like cars, but I have no business sense."

"What sense *do* you have?"

"I have a BA in Russian History. I *love* history. I'm thinking about going back to school and doing some more Eastern Europe."

"Did Bookman ever talk about his business? How he made his living?"

Dorman shook his head *no*. "We talked about cars and

women. I'm into blondes, he was hair-agnostic. But you should have seen the chick he brought to a meeting once. She had *huge* eyes. He got a phone call, so I started talking to her. Her accent was thick and western. When he got off the phone and called her name, she spun around, and I thought she was going to lose her balance because she was so top-heavy."

Grove smiled. "What did she talk about?"

"About her job at a bar. I think he brought her as eye candy. She never came to another meeting."

9:58 a.m.

"I'm sorry to have kept you waiting," John Mason said. He apologized to James and Joyce Bookman, who had been waiting for him since nine o'clock. "My shift normally starts at ten, but I could have been here at any time if I had known you were coming."

"We thought you would be here by eight o'clock," James said. His look said *Like a normal person.*

Officer Caligari, who had been babysitting the couple since nine o'clock, thought James should have apologized for not making an appointment. Instead, James merely sneered.

James kept talking. "I understand the need for you to hold the house and all of our son's property and assets. But do you know when we will be able to take possession and dispose of his things?"

Mason's lips twitched for a moment as he thought. "I wish," he said, "I wish I had a better idea when we'll be through. But this case is presenting uncommon challenges, things we almost never see in a murder investigation."

"What kind of challenges?"

"The absence of clear motive, for one. The lack of forensic evidence for another."

Joyce's voice rasped as she asked, "What was my son doing that an assassin would come after him? Was he selling drugs?"

"We have no indications of drug involvement," Mason said. "No drugs, paraphernalia, or excessive cash were found at his house. And his blood work came back clean as well. You saw the contents of his safe," John said. "The day we opened it was the first time we saw the contents, and it was only the kinds of legal papers that anyone would have."

"Could he have another safe?" James asked.

"If he had one, it's not in his house. We checked thoroughly."

Joyce asked, "Was he selling the bodies of those women — the ones from the funeral — as whores? They certainly *looked* the part, At least the one did. Has no one any decency anymore?"

"The one was not dressed in good taste," John said. "But there's no indication they were, as we say, 'working girls.' All the women who were there have regular lives and seem to be living within their apparent means."

"So, you're following up on everyone," James said. "Good. Most people are up to no good in some way."

"But almost no one commits murder," Mason said. "We look into most of them just enough to eliminate them from consideration."

"Very reasonable. But tell me something, Detective. Why were those FBI men at the house?"

"I wish I knew," John said. "They haven't told us why federal involvement is necessary. We are cooperating with them, but we believe this is purely a local police matter."

"Do they think you're out of your depth?"

Mason started slightly at the implication. His response was slow and measured. He was trying to avoid slugging James in the jaw. "All they have asked for so far is to be kept up to date on case progress, so they're getting a copy of everything as it comes in — the evidence reports, the interview reports, and so on."

It was time to get Mr and Mrs Bookman home and get back to work. "You have my assurance that we will keep you as up-to-date as we are able. You have my card — wait, let me get you another one."

John took a card from his pocket. "Here's my card, and on the back, I'm writing the number for my Lieutenant. Call me first if you need anything, but if I'm not available, call him."

The James and Joyce took the hint and stood. Joyce's cheeks were trembling.

After handshakes all around, Caligari walked them to the entrance nearest the visitors' parking.

When Caligari returned, she said, "You're a cruel man, Detective."

"Whatever could you *possibly* mean?"

"You know perfectly well what's going to happen when one of them asks for the lieutenant."

John chuckled softly and put on a way-out-in-the-country accent. "Yep, Lieutenant Tah-JEE-duh may not know what hit him."

10:46 a.m.

"Mrs Robinson?" the doctor said tentatively to the small, round-faced woman who held Jack Robinson's hand. He thought, *Except for the worry on her face, she would look twenty years too young to be married to him, white hair or no.*

"Yes." Robin looked up from where she sat by Jack's bed, holding his hand.

"We have the results of the cranial MRI. Your husband's condition is serious but stable. He has a concussion and possibly some bruising on his brain, and his neck and spine were twisted into a shape nature didn't intend."

"Stable is good, right?"

"Yes. We're going to keep him mostly under sedation for a couple of days at a minimum."

"His neck and spine ..."

"... were injured," the doctor said, "but he is not paralyzed. When he was conscious, he responded to pin pricks on his fingers and toes. Of course, we minimized the amount of movement, but he will require extensive physical therapy, and he will require surgery at some point. And his pain will be significant."

Robin looked at Jack's hand, his face, the brace holding his back and neck immobilized.

"Thank you," she said.

"There is one other thing."

"Yes?"

"When he was conscious briefly, your husband said 'run dark' or something like that. Do you know what that means?"

Robin nodded. "Yes, it's about a family friend named Ron

— *Ron*, not *run*. I'll have to call his daughter back."

The doctor nodded. "Good. When you feel like talking to him, you can tell him. I don't know whether he will understand you, but sometimes hearing a loved one speak can relieve his stress, and no one knows why." He nodded toward the nurse. "Nurse McKnight will explain to you about how to call for help and the facilities here for family. We are going to do everything possible to help your husband get better."

"Thank you," Robin said again.

The nurse went over everything and repeated the doctor's assurances.

When she was alone with Jack, she said, "You could have just *told* me you didn't want to go to Mexico for our anniversary."

After a few moments of quiet tears of sadness and relief and gratitude, Robin called Whit Thomas, their pastor; then she called Jack's brother, George; finally, she called Lenna Penfield.

"What can I do?" Lenna said through her tears.

"Pastor Thomas is on his way here," Robin said, "and I'll tell him about your father. I'm sure he'll be there as soon as he can."

Though Robin couldn't see it, Lenna nodded. "The pastor came yesterday, but it didn't go well," she said finally. "I guess that's the way it is."

11:54 a.m.

Alcalá drifted into the bullpen, stumbling and envying Atlas. His feet weren't dragging, but had he had a tail, it would have been.

"You look like hell, Mark," Mason observed.

Alcalá looked at him, focused, and said, "Thanks. Thanks a lot."

"Are you okay?"

Mark shook his head. "Rough night."

This was a first. Some mornings he was more awake than others, but he hadn't looked this sick before. Or was he ...

"Hung over?"

Mark nodded.

Mason fished three dollars out of his pocket and tossed them to Mark. "Get all the water from the machine this will buy. Drink it all in the next fifteen minutes."

"That's a lot. And fast."

"Yep. Do you take aspirin?"

"Yeah, but I don't have any."

Mason tossed Mark a bottle, and the pills rattled as Mark caught it.

"Take three."

Mark looked up, his irises barely edging out the bloodshot lines.

Mason said, "It's either this or go home. And this is the last time I pay."

Mark nodded and mumbled, "Cheers," set down the aspirin bottle, and shuffled off to the drink machine.

Mason blinked, wondering, then shook his head and picked up the medical examiner's final report. It was practically identical to the preliminary report: Slight irritation of the nasal passages, regular dose of Benadryl in his blood, gunshot wound in his head. The body exhibited no signs of a struggle, and probably wasn't moved after being shot — it was certainly in the same position as he had fallen.

Mason closed the folder and set the report on Mark's desk. He picked up the final forensics report next.

Mark meandered back in carrying two water bottles by the neck between the fingers of his right hand, which hung by his side.

"Quaff one of those, then look over the ME's final report."

Mark nodded and complied, taking the aspirin with the first swallow. After a couple of minutes he said, "No surprises here. What's next?"

"Look over the forensics final."

Mark was looking at the quantitative data, things like the amount of hair in various parts of Nathan Bookman's house. He was barely conscious when Mason's phone rang, startling him.

Mason answered. He listened for a moment then said, "Is there any doubt about the ID? ... No? ... Okay. Is that in Fulton or DeKalb? ... D'you know who the detective in charge is? ... Okay, thanks. I'll get that from the local PD."

"What's up?" Mark asked.

Mason thought he sounded funny — almost out of breath.

"The woman you interviewed, Ruth Sellers — she just turned up dead in the west end of Decatur."

Mark finished the second bottle of water around the same time as the second report. "Be back in a minute."

A couple of minutes later, he reappeared with a coffee cup in his hand.

"That smells awful," Mason said. "You should have made a new pot."

"I started one," Mark said. "But I went ahead and got this because even if the caffeine doesn't keep me awake, maybe the taste will."

Mason nodded. *One day*, he thought, *I'll have to get him a cup of whatever Ron Penfield makes.*

2:33 p.m.

Ron found Robin Robinson in the waiting room outside the Intensive Care Unit. An elderly man sat off to one side.

"Robin, I'm so sorry Jack was hurt. What happened?"

Robin stared at Ron, her face growing red with fury, sorrow, worry.

"What?" Ron asked, his guard rising reflexively.

"If you ..." Robin began. "He was on his way to see *you*, Ron."

"What? Why?"

"Because your daughter cares more about you than you apparently do yourself. She called Jack to come by because *you* were 'shaded' or something, and he left his job site to go and talk with *you*."

Her words hung in the air as she fixed her eyes on his. She looked like she wanted to swat him out of existence.

"I ... I ... I didn't know," Ron said, aghast. "Why would Lenna ... wait. 'Shaded?' or 'dark'?"

Robin's face softened, slowly, as she absorbed Ron's question.

" 'Dark', I think."

A nurse appeared at the door of the waiting room. "Mrs Robinson? Mr Robinson is awake for the next few minutes, if you'd like to see him."

Robin stood and relaxed visibly. She glanced sidelong at Ron before disappearing behind the nurse through the wide automatic doors.

Ron had forgotten the older man, who said, "Man," his voice deep and sonorous, with a hint of an Irish accent. "Whatever she thinks you did, I hope you didn't."

Ron said, "Thanks. I didn't do it, but I started the chain of events that got us here."

"Choices," the man said. "Everybody makes them. Some lead to good results; some to bad. Sometimes it's hard to know where it will lead. 'Ambition, the soldier's virtue, rather makes choice of loss, than gain which darkens him.'"

"That's just what I was trying to do!" Ron said. "I made a choice to try to help someone then it backfired and my wife died and I keep feeling like if I had chosen differently — had chosen the easier path — she'd still be alive." A crease appeared between Ron's eyebrows. "Shakespeare?"

The man nodded and stuck out a hand. "Darragh O'Connor."

Ron shook his hand. "Ron Penfield."

"I know. I taught English to high schoolers who didn't want to learn it, and I still pay attention to news about schools and teachers. I recognized you from the news coverage last year."

Ron grimaced.

"You said, 'chain of events'," Darragh said. "You made a choice at the beginning, yes?"

"Yes, one that continued for several months until I had to make another choice, one that . . . made her — the girl — want revenge."

"Your choices were your choices. You didn't *make* her do anything. *She* chose to sabotage your wife's car. *She* chose revenge. *She* chose even the desire that soured into revenge.

195

She chose. Not you."

A short, stout young woman with flaming red hair appeared at the door. "What are *you* doing here?" she shot across the room to Mr O'Connor.

"Can I not see my granddaughter, Aoife? My only grand-child?"

"Aoife?" Ron said. "What's happened?"

"Mister Penfield," she said. "Estrella is ill with a bacterial infection. I'm sorry you have to see our family brokenness."

To Darragh, she said, " *You* broke that line of contact years ago, Father. Since you insulted Callum. In front of his parents, no less. You should go before he sees you."

"Aoife, please! I was wrong." Tears streamed down his face. "Can we not choose better today?"

Aoife stared at his hair, his face, his tears, and she inhaled and exhaled. And again. "Wait here."

Darragh waited at the door, staring toward the ICU wing.

Without looking at Ron, Darragh asked, "You know Aoife?"

Ron started at his question. "We go to church together. Aoife, Wiley, and their kids. And Robin — that was Robin who's unhappy with me — her husband is one of our elders." Silently he prayed for the family's reconciliation.

Finally, apparently responding to a signal from farther down the hall, Darragh took a hesitating step toward the wing. His second step was firmer, by the time he passed out of Ron's sight, he was almost running.

It's easy, Ron thought, *to abstract away bad events until it happens to someone close to you.*

6:04 p.m.

"We've been real proud of you, Marco." The Handler spoke to him on the phone. "Message I got says it's time for you to come home."

At his end, Mark's eyes grew wide. "Really? I've done hardly anything."

"I know it feels like that. I just relay the message."

"Have I done something wrong?"

"No, Marco. No! You've stuck to your cover — the temptation is always there, no matter how good it is — but you made it work. You've hit your appointed jobs, excelled at them, never raised any suspicion. You've fed back the information requested. You hit the trifecta, and they want to reward you for it."

"So why not leave me here? Why not let me keep doing the job if I'm so good at it?"

"I can only guess, but there was something about teaching. Maybe they want you to teach new people how to keep a cover going."

Mark considered this. In his own mind his performance was unremarkable. He took a deep breath.

"So, what do I do?"

The Handler gave him instructions for the pickup that night, and he explained about his flight the following Tuesday and a few instructions for the intervening days.

"What do I do the rest of the time?"

"Whatever you want. Have a good time. Just change your look the way I told you and stay away from Bristow."

As they rang off, Mark was at once elated and frightened.

He had never been to Minsk; his parents emigrated while his mother was pregnant with him, claiming political oppression. The Canadian government had bought it.

The young parents raised Nikolai in a Kingston suburb, running a bar frequented by Canadian Army and Air Force officers, feeding names of the discontented to other agents who fished for information or, occasionally, recruits.

At age sixteen, when Nikolai was selected for his own assignment, he was tested and trained in spycraft at an isolated farm outside Minneapolis. His cover story was established via the resident cover family, the Alcalás. They owned a house and cars, had credit cards, bank accounts, took vacations, had birth records, death certificates, grades from school. They were doing this long before the Soviet breakup. "Mark" was the name they had reserved for him.

And the Handler was right: even though Mark hadn't done much in his own perception, he *had* kept his cover secure on the police force, working his way from recruit to uniform to detective. *I can handle a new identity for a few days. Easy.*

10:03 p.m.

As instructed, Mark waited on a downtown Atlanta street corner, just down the block from his pickup truck. Over his jeans and golf shirt, he wore a jacket against the rain that had blown in late in the afternoon. The forecast promised a few cooler days; it wouldn't go above eighty-five again until Thursday, and he'd be long gone.

This particular part of downtown was filled with buildings of ten stories or more. Typical of downtown Atlanta late on a

Saturday evening, no one was around. Even all the Starbucks were closed.

Mark saw someone come around the next corner to the northeast and walk toward him, then duck into a recessed doorway. Mark walked that way and into the doorway. He and the other exchanged pass phrases, then the man handed him a backpack and returned the way he came.

Examining the contents, Mark saw that everything was exactly as he had been told: a Kentucky driver's license and another one from West Virginia with a different name; a passport matching the license from West Virginia; two credit cards (one for either identity); a stack of cash; a cell phone; an airline boarding pass for Tuesday in the West Virginia name. Pictures on the IDs were both of him, but the West Virginia documents had been Photoshopped to resemble what his appearance would be in a couple of days. Everything was covered with a layer of dirty clothes. He didn't count the cash, but he guessed it was about five thousand. *He said I could have a good time.*

As instructed, Mark walked southwest a block to the corner of Marietta Street then northwest. As he crossed North Avenue by the Georgia Tech campus, he realized he'd have to call a cab to make one last V-run. There isn't a Varsity in Minsk.

When he rounded the campus on the west side, no one noticed him. In the misty streetlight he looked like any ordinary college student with a backpack.

Half a mile up, he followed the right fork onto Northside Drive, stopping long enough to remove his jacket. The rain had driven the humidity up and he was sweating. He was going to be picked up somewhere on Northside Drive — or was it Northside Parkway? He hoped it was Drive; the Parkway was about six miles farther up.

He stopped at a convenience store and found plastic bags — way overpriced, but with five grand in his pocket, he didn't care — and put the cell phone in it to protect it from the rain. He wasn't likely to need it; it was just a precaution against unforeseen problems.

He mentally reviewed his instructions as he walked: After being picked up, he'd be taken to a hotel. He'd check in as the Kentuckian, stay overnight, then check out and take a cab to a hairdresser. He'd pay cash to get his hair died and restyled, then go buy a nice suit with the West Virginia credit card. In his West Virginia persona and new clothes, Mark would check into a different hotel. Generally speaking, he was to be visible and innocuous.

And no longer Mark Alcalá.

A couple of blocks before the interstate, a car stopped alongside him. The window was down, and he saw a familiar face inside. It was his Handler.

"What's your name?"

"Call me Leif." Mark gave the name on the Kentucky driver's license.

"Need a lift, Leif?"

"Sure." Mark put his bag into the back seat and climbed in.

"Where you headed?"

"Just up to Smyrna. How far can you take me?"

"If it's close to U.S. 41, I can put you on the doorstep."

They smiled as only co-conspirators can.

They continued on up Northside rather than getting on the interstate. "Why this way?" Mark — now Leif — asked.

"We're not in a hurry, and I figured we could chat. In all

your years here, we've only been face-to-face a couple of times. What can you tell me about your objective? I'm going to need to pass your intel off to your successor."

Leif outlined what he knew: One of the FBI guys had mentioned the warehouse once, and Mason had noticed but hadn't said anything; the surveillance video hadn't shown anyone entering or leaving; the only people around were the twenty-four-hour security monitors. The monitors themselves were usually college kids, never slept on duty, didn't have access to the inside of the warehouse, mostly monitored the video, motion sensors, and doors and skylights, never played videos or loud music.

"The only way you're going to get into that building is to have them let you in."

The Handler nodded. Mark — *Leif,* he corrected himself, was a good observer. The police training had improved his skills. A shame, really.

They went on talking, about police training; detective classes; what Minsk was going to be like — summer wasn't bad, but Leif would need some heavier clothes for winter.

Leif said he knew the drill from growing up in Canada and Minnesota.

Then he asked, "You aren't from Minsk, like my parents were. How did you get involved?"

The Handler sighed as he thought for a minute. It wasn't going to matter if he told him. "My daddy used to drink and beat me and my mamá, and he showed me that honest people are the ones who suffer, him not being one. So I wrote something about that in a college English class, and my professor noticed and started talking me up."

Lief nodded and smiled, "From growing up with my parents, I bet I'd recognize that conversation."

"Eventually, they got me a fake passport and a plane ticket, and I flew to Vienna and took trains to Minsk. After they found me reliable, they trained me and sent me back. I never finished college, and I wound up here."

As they rounded the curve onto Northside Parkway, the Handler said, "I'm not really taking you to the door of the hotel. We're going to stop a couple of blocks short of the river, and you'll walk the rest of the way."

Leif looked a little disappointed, but he nodded and said "Okay."

As Leif looked through the wall of giant trees on the passenger side, the Handler twisted a bit of brightly colored foam rubber between the thumb and forefinger of his opposite hand. He inserted it into his ear and began twisting another piece of foam.

As promised, they stopped just in sight of the bridge across the Chattahoochee.

"It's been good working with you, 'Leif'."

They shook hands, and Alcalá turned away and got out.

The Handler quickly inserted the foam piece into the other ear, then reached into the pocket on his door.

When Leif leaned in to say goodbye, he faced the cap on the end of a piece of white pipe with a half-inch hole drilled in it. The pipe was attached to a small handgun.

He fell with a hole in his forehead.

The Handler knew he had little time, and moved quickly: A roll of plastic from the trunk, wrap the body, back into the trunk. Then drive — west on the I-285 bypass, then northwest on I-85, then I-985. He exited just south of Lake Lanier, and worked his way back over to the Hootch, through a neighborhood that had private tennis courts a hundred yards from the river. He drove in slowly, lights off.

Another car pulled in — Jury's car. Good — no one was around.

They had practiced this move a few months ago, well before they knew Alcalá would be their bundle. At the bank of the river, they unwrapped the body and rolled it into the water.

Bundling the plastic back into the trunk, Mark-Leif's (former) Handler drove fifteen minutes back to the interstate and another thirty minutes northeast, just past the end of the reservoir, and then into a neighborhood right by the river; he threw the gun and the homemade suppressor into the river.

At the next exit, he drove into an industrial park and ditched the plastic in a dumpster. Finally, he sprayed the interior of his car and his trunk with Febreze. In a couple of days he'd take his car for interior detailing, which should get rid of gunshot residue.

But his night wasn't over yet. He and Jury drove back to Alcalá's apartment complex, parking on the far side. They walked separate routes through the maze of apartments and met at the front door. Donning rubber gloves and paper surgical scrubs, they entered using a key the Handler had gotten from Mark the first time they met. They gathered every bit of electronics: TV, cell phone, computer, everything.

They unscrewed every outlet cover and light switch cover to look inside, checking behind each other before reinstalling them; they pulled the refrigerator, range and dishwasher away from the walls, and checked backs and walls and every compartment; dumped the ice from the ice maker and examined every piece of ice.

They found Alcalá's emergency credentials in a magnetic key holder on the back of the refrigerator; and that was all they found.   Other than what might be on the electronics, Alcalá's apartment was completely clean. He had followed his training well.

By the time they finished, it was almost six a.m.

They stowed all the things they had gathered into two large backpacks and left about five minutes apart.

Saturday, June 30

Mason heard his phone ringing in the car as he approached it. Captain Berman was on the other end.

"Captain, what do you need?"

"Whatever you're doing, drop it and get back here now. And from now on, I'd better not have to call four times to get hold of you."

"Yes, sir. I'll be there in fifteen or less."

"Make it less."

Mason was saying "Will do" as the captain rang off.

Twelve minutes later, Mason was at Berman's door.

"John, have you heard anything at all from Detective Alcalá?"

"Not since yesterday. What's going on?"

Berman shook his head. "Mark's body washed up in the Chattahoochee under the bridge at McGinnis Ferry Road."

"What do we know?"

"He was waterlogged, and he had a hole in his forehead."

Mason blinked twice and closed his eyes. "The same as Bookman."

Berman nodded.

Mason blinked back tears. There would be time for grief later.

"Who's got the scene?"

"Fulton County police. I talked with the north Fulton major, Olson, and they're giving us full access. I want you to be on top of it. You can get whatever help you need, rearrange anyone's schedule. Anything at all."

"Thanks. Do you want a list?"

Berman grabbed a pencil. "Shoot."

"I need warrants for a bunch of stuff: Mark's apartment, car, locker. I need a second forensics team at his apartment. Has his car been found?"

"Not yet."

"We have to find it. I need someone from the Medical Examiner's office to go with me to the Fulton ME's. Did he have direct deposit?"

"Don't know. Almost everyone does." Berman held up a finger as he caught up on the note taking. "Go," he said.

"We need access to his bank, credit card, utilities, cell phone, Internet if he had it. We need his address book. Oh, and while we're waiting for warrants, I'm going to get someone on his desk and computer here."

Berman nodded as he continued writing. "Anything else?"

"I'll let you know."

As Mason was headed back to his desk, Lieutenant Tejeda stuck his head out the door of his office. "Mason, I just heard about Mark. The captain is right to give you the lead. Hand off the peripheral stuff to me, and we'll feed you information as we get it."

"Thanks. I gave the captain a list of warrants I need, if you can get that from him and get started on it, that would be a big help."

Tejeda nodded.

"I'm going to need computer forensics help. Do I call the county for that?"

"For his desk computer?"

Mason nodded. "Also, we should treat his desk as a source of evidence. I'll call Welch. And where is Crosley? I need document forensics on all his papers."

"Vacation." Tejeda thought for a minute. "O'Kelly — he took the classes after his arm got shot up so he could be active until he could take retirement. I'll call him. Did he know Mark?"

"I think so — I think they overlapped a few months when Mark was in uniform. And O'Kelly is a good choice." Mason went on. "I'm going to North Fulton with someone from the ME's office for a look-see at the body. I'm going to try to get permission to participate in the autopsy."

Tejeda acknowledged that Mason was steps in the right order and headed to the Captain Berman's office to get the warrant list.

Mason went over everything in his mind as he draped Alcalá's desk in yellow tape. He called Welch and told her what he needed, then went to the locker room to similarly decorate the young detective's locker.

Warrants streamed in over the next half hour. Welch had about half of Alcalá's stuff bagged and labeled when the warrant came for his apartment. She handed off the remainder of the desk and Alcalá's locker to an assistant, then took the rest of her team to his apartment. With the warrant for financials and phone, detective Garcia started down those paths.

A phone call gave Mason the schedule for the body's autopsy. Fulton was fast-tracking it (relatively) since Mark was a police officer, but they wouldn't get started until Monday morning.

10:04 a.m.

Mason hung up his desk phone. And inhaled and exhaled long breaths. Twice. Everything had just shifted under his feet again.

"Michael," he said, "what do you have going right now?"

Michael Renfroe looked up. "Just a couple of B-and-E cases. What do you need?"

"Take an hour and hand them off. I've got three murders, one or two perps. I need your eyes."

Renfroe glanced at the two stacks of paper on his desk. He riffled either stack once and said, "Be with you in thirty minutes."

Mason nodded. He picked up his phone and dialed an internal number. No answer. He dialed another number. "Johnson, this is Mason. You busy? ... Yeah ... Bring a van and a high-resolution camera with a tripod. We're going back to Nathan Bookman's house. ... What happened? We just found out where to look. When can you leave? ... Okay."

While Renfroe worked his way through handing off his cases, Mason was letting Lieutenant Tejeda and Captain Berman know how he had to rearrange the coordination of the cases.

"Bookman's murder is the key to the whole thing," he told them. "I need my personal primary attention there." He went on to explain the phone call he had just received. They agreed with his assessment, and the lieutenant took on coordination of Alcalá's case.

Half an hour later, Renfroe had handed his cases off to other officers.

"So, what's up, John?"

Mason handed him three summary folders, the kind he kept current for briefing the Captain or the Loo. "The first and third are almost certainly by the same perpetrator. The MOs are identical."

"And the second?"

"Similar. We've got to roll in forty-five minutes. I want to talk in the car on the way."

Renfroe opened the top one. "Nathan Bookman. Same guy from the Jamison case?"

"Yeah. Never implicated though."

Renfroe put ear buds in and dialed his player to loud music. He pursed his lips, half-closed his eyes, and lit into the pile of paper.

Mason dialed an external number. "This is Detective Mason. Can you meet us in an hour? Great. See you then."

He typed an update email for Lieutenant Tejeda, copied to Captain Berman. Then he sat and thought through what he knew.

Renfroe finished the first two folders in twenty-five minutes and opened the third. When he saw the name, he pulled his ear buds and pushed his chair back. "Whoa! Alcalá?"

Mason nodded.

Renfroe pushed his ear buds back in and pored over the

file.

When it was five minutes before time to leave, he went to the men's room and then got a soft drink from the machine. Riding with Mason, he said, "Okay, where do we start?"

When he started to open his drink, Mason gave him the furry eyeball.

"Sorry, I forgot."

He held the plastic bottle by the lid for the remainder of the ride.

"So, what do we have, John?"

"That phone call," Mason said, "right before I asked you to hand off your cases: It was from the company that installed Nathan Bookman's safe."

Renfroe nodded. "Yeah, the file said he thought something was weird, but he didn't know what."

"The guy said he had talked with someone at a security company in Chattanooga who had heard from someone about alterations made to the same model. It gives a way to hide extra papers — three or four sheets at most."

"How does it work?"

"You'll see that when we get there. The security guy will show us how. Lanny Johnson is meeting us."

"What about calling in the feds? Your two FBI guys, or maybe the beak-nosed woman or Stolzfus? If Bookman really was involved with the Senator's doings, this could provide confirmation, additional client lists, or trails to offshore money."

Mason nodded. "Good idea. Call Fussy now and tell him we may have something."

"What about the FBI guys?"

"I called them just before you finished with the files, but they were near Columbus and won't be here for the safe opening."

The corners of Mason's mouth twitched.

"You look disappointed."

"Oh yeah," Mason said with mock distress. "It's killing me."

Renfroe placed the call to the Federal prosecutor. After he rang off, he said, "Stolzfus said to go ahead, but make sure he gets a copy of everything."

Mason nodded as they pulled into Bookman's driveway, and Johnson pulled up to the curb in the forensics van from the opposite direction.

Johnson met them in the driveway.

"Hey Lanny," Renfroe said.

"Hey Michael. What do I need to bring in, John?"

"Depends on the security guy."

Renfroe finally opened his drink and took a sip, grimacing at the relative warmth of it.

Mason saw him. "You could have driven yourself," he said.

Renfroe said, "You wanted to talk in the car," just as the Ribo Security's SUV drove up. Alton Williams got out, and Mason introduced him to his colleagues.

Mason unlocked the door, and everyone walked to the end of the hall that contained the safe.

Mason said, "Can you explain what you told me on the phone, maybe filling in the details?"

"Sure," Williams said. "I was talking with a friend from Chattanooga who installs safes. Like Ribo, he installs a lot of this particular model. He told me about a client, a paranoid old geezer, who had modified his safe to make sure his son-in-law couldn't get to some of his most valuable papers: a deed and a rare, negotiable bond."

As Williams spoke, Mason, Renfroe, and Johnson donned

gloves.

"The client hired someone to make an impression of the back of the safe: the back inch or so of the top, bottom, left, and right sides, and the entire back."

"How was the impression made?" Johnson asked.

"With spray-on silicon rubber. When the impression was removed, it was used to mold a new back for the safe."

"Wouldn't the rubber be too fragile?"

"Yeah, my friend said the guy doing the alteration took three times to get it right. When the hidden papers were in place, a piece of very thin metal was pressed in place, sealed around the edges, and painted. While the paint was tacky the impression was pressed in place to make the texture look right."

Renfroe asked, "How much stuff did the old guy get back there?"

"Four sheets of fairly thick paper."

Mason asked, "Why did the client tell your friend about it?"

Williams tapped his forefingers together, alternating one over the other several times. "He said the client thought the guy doing the alterations seemed fishy, and that he wanted a witness for what he put in the safe. The installer's bond gave the client a better feeling about the legitimacy of the whole thing."

Renfroe grinned. "I bet the alterations guy does work for others who aren't completely legal."

"Could be. Not my business."

Mason asked, "So what is the back made of?"

"It was a plate of steel, the same alloy as the safe interior is made of and painted with the same paint as well."

"How thick is it?"

"Bobby — my pal in Chattanooga — said it was maybe three sixty-fourths of an inch."

"So, if there's anything in the safe at all, even an expert like you would have a hard time noticing it — like everyone else, you would look at the contents, not the safe itself."

Williams nodded. "When we first opened this safe, it was after you had taken the contents out that I realized — more like felt like — something wasn't right. Now I know what it is: The interior isn't deep enough."

Johnson asked, "So assuming this was done the same way, what do we need to do to open it?"

"Just an X-Acto knife, or something similar. There's a thin bead of clear silicon rubber around the edges of the safe's back, textured and painted to match the back and sides, and to obscure the alteration."

While Williams opened the safe and removed the shelves, Johnson set his toolbox down and got out a knife. Setting a small light and magnifier on the floor of the safe, Johnson said, "It appears to be exactly as you described."

Johnson ran the knife around the edge of the safe's back, being careful not to go too deep. As he finished the last edge, he said, "Could someone hand me two small suction cups?"

Renfroe found them in the toolbox, and Johnson pressed them into the back, near the top right and bottom left corners. Everyone held their breath as he pulled gently. Nothing happened for a few seconds, then the lower left cup popped off.

"Okay," Johnson said, "I'm going to scrape this silicone rubber off with the knife. Michael, will you hold a bag open to collect it in?"

Renfroe nodded and got an evidence bag out while Johnson pulled the seal out in six pieces, two from either side and one

213

each from top and bottom. He dropped them in the bag and nodded, and Renfroe sealed the bag and wrote the required information on the label.

Johnson re-engaged the lower left suction cup and pulled gently on both of them. After a brief hesitation the steel plate came out. Mason slid it into an evidence bag.

Three sheets of paper fell down from the back of the safe. Johnson let them fall face down onto one gloved hand, supporting them with outstretched fingers.

They all walked slowly to the dining room, where Johnson spread the papers out.

"My part of this is over," Williams said. "Is it okay if I go on? I have a service call to make in Alpharetta."

"Sure," Mason said. "Michael, will you go with him to lock the safe?"

Renfroe did so, and then Mason & Johnson said goodbye to Williams as Renfroe followed him to the door.

"Lanny, I need high-resolution photos of all three sheets, front and back. That's your number one priority. Number two is thorough examination for any weirdness at all — ink that only shows up in black light, and so on. Number *three* is standard exam for fingerprints and other telltale latent evidence."

Johnson nodded and went to his van. When he returned, he had a tripod and a digital camera. He set the camera up on the dining room table. He returned to his van, and came back with a couple of stands that had small lights at the top.

"I'm worried about heat from these lights, Lanny."

"That's not a problem," Johnson said. "These are LED lights. They're very efficient and make almost no heat. They'll be common in a few years."

He finished adjusting the lights and said, "Okay, here's the plan: I'm going to take two pictures of everything on two separate memory cards. One card goes to you, the other goes to evidence."

"Do you have to account for the card?"

"We misplace these things sometimes and have to replace them. Just takes a trip to Best Buy or someplace — they're common consumer-type cards."

Mason nodded thanks, recognizing the extra copy as a favor.

Pictures done, Johnson gingerly inserted the pages into clear plastic bags. As he put his equipment away, Mason finally got a look at them up close.

The first page contained ten handwritten rows of entries; each entry had three items: 4 numbers separated by periods, a 13-digit number, and a string of 8 to 10 seemingly random characters.

Mason glanced at Renfroe. "What do you think?"

Renfroe shook his head. "Too easy," he said. "IP address, account number, password. Ten different accounts and the access to them."

"Just what I was thinking. Stolzfus gets that one."

The second page contained only a set of cryptic directions: "Aisle 3, Shelf 15, Box 4. Paper copy, marked Top Secret / Striation Access Only."

"Top Secret sounds important," Renfroe said.

"More important is the 'Striation' endorsement. That's a designation for a special access program. It means that in addition to your clearance, you have to have permission to have a need to know. And then you can only get to it if you actually need to know."

"What do you think it was?"

Mason just shook his head and moved to the third sheet.

"If something should happen to me," it read, "please understand that I believe I am in danger. I am threatened by agents of a foreign government."

And that was all it said.

Mason put his thumb and forefinger on either side of the bridge of his nose and closed his eyes.

Renfroe blinked and said, "What —" He cut himself off when Mason held up the forefinger of his free hand.

They stood there silently until Johnson returned a moment later for his second load.

"Lanny," Mason said, pointing at the third sheet, "this one is your top priority. Check it under ultraviolet light, polarized light, anything you can think of before applying chemicals. Michael, let's help Lanny with his equipment and get him on the road right now."

They did so, and Johnson drove away.

Mason asked, "Do you have duty all next week?"

Renfroe shook his head no. "We were going to the mountains for a couple of days, Wednesday and Thursday. If you want, I can eat the deposit."

"I need you to do that. And tell Constance I'm sorry. But you can come to the party on Wednesday if we have it; I'll let you know if it is canceled."

12:17 p.m.

Grove and Orozco drove through downtown Atlanta, headed north after turning up exactly nothing. Orozco drove; Grove's phone rang.

"Mason," Grove said, "Have you got something?"

"Yes, I have something, and it puts the Bookman case squarely into your jurisdiction."

"Hold on a second." Grove pressed a button on the phone. "Okay, Orozco and I are on speaker. What have you got?"

"We got a call from the security company that installed Bookman's safe."

"And?"

Mason described what they had found and described the contents of the three hidden notes.

Grove asked, "Who have you told about this?"

"My captain, my forensics guy, and another detective who was here with us. I sent the bank account info to Boris Stolzfus in the federal prosecutor's office. I'm betting it's related to the Jamison case. And I have photographs of the papers."

"Can your people be trusted?"

"Yes, without reservation."

Orozco asked, "Is the evidence being handled properly?"

"Without question."

"Can you send us copies of the papers? Send them to my email account. We have a laptop in the car with a cell connection."

Grove pulled the computer from the back seat and got it going as they talked.

"It'll be on the way seconds after we hang up. We took very

high-resolution photos — do you want me to shoot them down to, say, two hundred PPI?"

"That's fine, as long as it's fast and readable."

"Hold on," Mason said.

The agents heard the clack of computer keys.

When the sound of Mason's typing paused, he said, "You'll think it's magic. Just one thing."

"What's that?"

"I want to be part of it. Whoever killed Bookman killed my partner, too. I want a piece of the arrest."

Orozco said, "I can't promise anything on the phone, but we'll let you know what we can do by the end of the day."

"Won't ask for more."

"One last thing," Grove said. "Vic and I need to talk in person with everyone who knows the content of these notes."

"The three of us are available. The security consultant didn't see the contents, so there's no problem there."

"We can't afford loose ends, John."

"This is what we've got."

"It'll have to do."

When the emails arrived, Grove and Orozco had almost reached I-285, the Atlanta bypass on the north side of town.

Grove said to his partner, "It's exactly what Mason said it is."

"Do you think the note tells the truth? About foreign agents? Or was Bookman hedging his bet?"

"No way to tell. But we may get something on his contact with ..."

"With who?" Orozco asked.

"My favorite has always been Belarus. Yours?"

"Moldova, maybe? Though they may not be stable enough to field a decent intel team."

As they crossed under a bridge, Orozco said, "Go ahead and refer all the stuff upstairs. Let them know what we're doing."

Grove nodded, then composed and sent the email.

10:06 p.m.

Roddy Noble sat at the watchman's desk in the secure warehouse facility. He had a hot date with his organic chemistry textbook, and he took notes as he went. A small speaker played Chopin études at a low volume. When the alarm chirped, he made a mental note to check it in a minute.

That minute stretched into ten.

When he finally looked up after completing a nasty equation, he remembered the alarm and started checking monitors. All six looked okay on first inspection, but according to the procedure, he was supposed to do the spot check.

All six cameras in the facility had a partial view of some piece of floor. When he pressed the button that corresponded to each camera, a small, weak laser — a common laser pointer — projected a beam onto a spot on the floor visible from the corresponding camera. If an intruder were to position a photo of the camera's view so the person monitoring couldn't see what was going on in the warehouse, the spot wouldn't appear on the monitor and the alarm could be raised. Occasionally a motion detector chirped when a rat crossed the floor or a bat crossed a skylight, and there was no problem.

The lasers were not next to the cameras but were set in the steel rafters near the ceiling at angles, so they wouldn't be obvious to the earthbound observer, almost thirty-five feet below.

The protocol demanded that Roddy perform the spot check when his shift started, and he had done so within three minutes of his arrival, just before cracking the textbook. He was also to check the spots every hour or so.

The security company, contracted by the federal government, which owned the facility, hired pre-med students with good grade averages because they could be relied on to follow procedure.

The chirp, a single tone sourced at an array of motion detectors, was a signal to perform the spot check immediately. The chemistry problem had been the only thing in Roddy's way, and he guessed it was a rat in the building anyway.

He pressed the button for the first camera, which was positioned to look from the side at the floor mat just inside the front door. Sure enough, a bright spot appeared on the floor a few inches from the main doorway.

Camera Two looked at the emergency exit door on one side of the building, near the back wall. Spot, yes; problem, no.

The remaining cameras looked down the main aisles that ran the length (Cameras Three and Four) and width (Cameras Five and Six) of the warehouse. Camera Three, okay. Camera Four, okay. Camera Five ... he pressed the button again. Camera Five ... nothing.

He was on the phone in ten seconds.

"This is Roderick Noble at the Fifth Street Magazine. We are failing a spot check."

Within three minutes, a sedan and a minivan pulled into the parking lot. Two Army MPs lit out of the sedan, four from the van. The two from the car walked around the building to the emergency door, while another pair made their way to the front door. The final pair went into the office and verified the failed check.

On a signal through their comms, Roddy turned on all the lights inside and outside the warehouse, and the MPs opened both front and back doors, firearms at the ready. As the lights came up, they swept the rows of shelves simultaneously from both directions, meeting in the middle.

Nothing.

The pair in the office exited and began a sweep of the fence around the facility.

The MPs could see all six laser spots when they were activated. But Roddy still didn't see the spot for Camera Five, and that monitor still showed the lights off inside. When an MP stood where he should see her, he didn't.

All the cameras were checked, the MPs looking through binoculars. All appeared to be untouched.

The warehouse was constructed on a concrete slab that showed no signs of being dug up, so three members of the team headed for the outside ladder that led to the roof.

Engel had the key to the cage at the foot of the ladder, but when she reached it, the padlock had been cut off. Just after the alert went out to the squad, the MPs checking the perimeter called in to report a breach in the fence where the kudzu had grown up around some tree stumps. The whole squad went to a higher alert status.

As the squad was about to enter the cage to climb to the roof, Grove and Orozco drove up. Engel walked back over to meet them. They got out of their car and showed their credentials to her.

"I was told you were coming," she said. "How would you

like to work with us?"

Grove said, "I want to look around inside the warehouse."

Engel looked at Orozco.

"Let me look at the security control station," he said. "I need to see what the staffer there saw."

The squad began ascending the ladder.

Grove entered the warehouse and looked around. He had seen the security plans, so he went immediately to the southeast corner, which was overseen by Camera Five.

He called Orozco on his cell phone.

"What are you looking at, Vic?"

"I have a separate monitor for each camera feed. The one that failed to show the laser spot is still showing the warehouse is dark. Are the lights turned on in there?"

"Yep. It's as bright as day in here."

The security squad stood on the roof's solid perimeter, a strip of tar about two feet wide, looking onto the gravel that covered most of the roof.

Engel called in. "The roof looks okay."

Mills, the squad leader, who had stayed inside the warehouse, said, "Check the skylights to see if they've been opened."

"Hold on," Engel said, "I'm going to put on gloves so any fingerprints won't be disturbed."

"Roger that."

After a moment, Engel said, "The northeast skylight is fine."

"Northwest skylight is secure."

"Southwest is secure."

"Okay, southeast skylight, the hatch is definitely not secured. The padlock has been cut open. Is there a ladder on the inside wall there?"

"Affirmative," Mills said. He stood at the foot of the ladder, which consisted of metal bars built into the wall. There was a similar ladder by each skylight. And someone coming in that way would be seen by Camera Five.

Mills was on his cell phone. "We need company B out here for a thorough sweep of the building," he said. "We definitely had an intruder here."

Hours later, Company B's detailed inspection of the building turned up exactly nothing. The boxes were inventoried, and all were confirmed present. Only one was unsealed, but it contained only office supplies.

Bolt cutters, about two feet long, were found a few yards from the building, tossed into the kudzu that covered the ground and the trees on the back side of the building.

The FBI agents, accompanied by a soldier, traced the wiring that ran from the misbehaving camera. Just where it entered the security office, the coaxial wire had been cut, and a breadboarded circuit was spliced in. An extra bit of wire fell off the end of the breadboard.

What Roddy had seen on monitor five was an image stored on the device from the camera, and it was fed in constantly. If a motion monitor hadn't detected movement, the change wouldn't have been detected until Roddy's next periodic spot check.

Roddy was given two weeks off to "concentrate on his studies," weeks he hadn't asked for or budgeted for.

Sunday, July 1

4:00 p.m.

When news of the warehouse break-in reached Grove and Orozco's supervisor, the FBI requested and (after dancing a round with the Army Criminal Investigation Division and then the Defense Criminal Investigative Service) got authority to investigate the incident.

Given the inventory of defunct, classified programs that had been temporarily stored, untouched, in the warehouse for the last six to twelve years, they had their hands full. A small army of FBI forensics specialists and investigators was called in.

Evidence on site showed that someone had inserted the video buffer in the circuitry at a place where the wiring was exposed but out of sight of the person working in the office. The wire hanging from the circuit was an antenna. Subsequent examination would show that when activated remotely, a video frame was grabbed and then substituted for the live feed from

225

the camera in the warehouse.

A small piece torn from an ordinary exam glove, the type sold by any drugstore, was found on the ground near where the electronics were inserted, but no fingerprints were found on it.

Grove and Orozco were in their own element at last.

FBI auditors were called in — it was a bit of an effort to find enough who had sufficient security clearances — and started checking. At Grove's insistence, they started in the corner of the building housing the material from Kaiser Transceivers.

And across the two days it took to do the inventory, everything seemed to be in place. Except for the box of office supplies, all seals on the containers were intact, each seal confirmed by three auditors who didn't know each other. The unsealed box was not in the Kaiser area, but from a laser system integrator that had gone out of business a year before Kaiser. The inventory record for that one read, "MISC. DESK CONTENTS," and it turned out to be exactly that: A stapler, a tape dispenser, scissors, paper clips, a few Dilbert printouts, and so on.

"Why bother?" Grove asked.

Orozco shuffled some papers. "The file says the company was shuttered by court order and everyone was searched on the way out."

"What was the address of the box?"

"Aisle 3, shelf 15, box 4." Something clicked in both of their minds at the same time. "Wait ..."

Grove went outside to make a call. When Mason answered, Grove said, "We thought we had the answer to the aisle 3 problem, but it was nothing."

"What happened?"

"There's a warehouse on Fifth street."

"Yeah, I was one of the people who moved the Kaiser stuff in there when we shut down."

"There was a break in, and the only container in the place that was opened was the one on that paper."

"What was in it?"

"Office supplies. And it wasn't in the area with the Kaiser boxes, but another company's stuff. Got any ideas?"

Mason tapped the edge of his phone with one finger. "Bookman was a mathematician. Try permuting the numbers."

"How many combinations does that make?"

"Six. Swap aisle, shelf, and box numbers around in the five remaining orders. See if that lands you anywhere in the Kaiser area. There may be more than one, and if this was Striation access, you're going to need some very high-altitude permission to look at it."

"How high?"

"Take a spacesuit and extra oxygen."

7:06 p.m.

Ann handed John the checklist.

He looked over it and nodded. "This is pretty complete," he said.

"I kept a copy of last year's list and the last-minute corrections to it. I didn't want to have to go through that again."

"It was mostly my fault," John acknowledged.

"Sure, and we had a lot of help finishing it off. I knew you were frustrated by that, so I figured this would help."

"Thanks. Without this, we'd probably have to call it off."

"Because of Mark?"

John nodded. "And the other case, Nathan Bookman. I offered cancellation to Captain Berman, but he insisted that we go ahead. 'We need to relax,' he said. 'Two murders, and one of them one of ours, has everyone on edge, but it's not the kind of edge that increases their efficiency or their clarity. John, we *need* your cookout to let off some steam,' he said."

Two years previous, John and Ann had hosted their first Fourth of July picnic for their coworkers and friends. The next year — last year — it had grown to four times the size, and they had barely been able to pull it off. This year, it was still going to be close.

John said, "I'll get a couple of guys to pick up the meat and a lot of the other supplies at Costco or wherever they are members. When I get it from them at work, I'll have a cooler with ice or dry ice to keep meat and other stuff cold until I can get home with it."

"That'll be a big help," Ann said. "I'm trying to land three big listings, and I won't be able to do much except on the day."

John nodded again. "Who are you going to invite besides the office folks?"

"I'll ask all three client couples to come. I think we can count on at least one to show up. You?"

"Whatever cops are off duty, plus the usual folks from Kaiser."

"Including Ron Penfield?

"Sure. He's been ... unreachable lately, but, hey, why not?"

"If there's even a *chance* he'll come, I don't think we could get Lisa McCloskey there with a hundred thousand dollar bonus."

"How do you think we should handle it? Do I leave him off the list?"

Ann drummed her fingers for a moment. "No," she said finally. "No, go ahead and invite him, but let me know whether he's coming so I can warn Lisa. After that business with Sean last fall ..."

"Yeah," John said, "I wouldn't blame her for staying away, either. Oh, and I'm going to invite the Donovans as well."

"Wait ... daughter who found herself pregnant, right? Her father was at Kaiser?"

"Yeah. Carlton works for the county now. I'm not sure what her mom does."

After a pause, Ann flicked a glance at John and then inhaled slowly.

"What is it?" he asked. "What do you want to say that you think I don't want to hear?"

"I think you should invite Lilia and Adena."

John's jaw bounced off the edge of the table and onto the floor. Across the next two full minutes, his face flushed, then drained of all color.

Ann waited patiently.

As his face was returning to its normal shade, John said, "I'll think about it."

He walked around the kitchen table, once, twice. Then he said, "Can we go for a walk?"

Ann nodded, and they both pocketed their cell phones and headed out.

Across the entire forty-five minutes of their wandering through their neighborhood, along the shopping and fast food drag between the entrances, and finally back to the house, neither of them said anything.

Back at home, Ann fetched slices of pizza — two for herself, three for John — from a storage bag in the refrigerator, put them on a stone cookie sheet, and set the cookie sheet into the oven. John got out a couple of glasses and a bottle of wine. Through it all, the silence lingered.

When Ann judged the pizza warm enough to eat, she retrieved it from the oven and transferred it to plates as John opened and poured the wine.

Finally, when John was halfway through his first slice, he whispered, "You're right, damn you. I'll call them tonight."

Ann nodded. John, she knew, was generally open-minded, and when she could present him with the right thing to do, he was honest enough that he could see it. Eventually.

John's ex-wife and their daughter might come, or they might not. But there would be another crack in the wall he had put up to try to close himself off from them.

As the room darkened from the setting sun, John's mood thawed, and they returned to their planning.

Ann had already bought the plastic table covers and put in the orders for the rented equipment and furnishings, and everything would be delivered late Tuesday. John would be responsible for setting everything up in their back yard; Ann would prepare hamburger patties, and so on. John would get the smoker going before he wen to bed on the third.

Finally, around ten 'til nine, all the planning was complete.

And John stared at his phone.

Sitting in his kitchen, he stared and blinked and breathed. He knew that when he picked up the phone, his life would change. And he liked his life. He liked his job; he loved his wife; he enjoyed his roses.

But Ann was right. It was time for a new stage in his life,

for redrawing the circle of his life to include his daughter. And, at least peripherally, his ex-wife.

He drew a deep breath and released it. And he picked up his phone.

One ring. Two. And that voice, that accent.

"Hello, John."

"Hi."

That hung in the air for a moment.

Until Lilia said, "Is there a reason you called, or are we going to only hang on speechless like we did for the last two years we were married?"

Might as well go for it, John thought. "How about this: We're having a big Independence Day gathering on Wednesday. Lots of people, some you will know from social events at Kaiser."

"You are sure it is not an imposition?"

"Not in the slightest. There will be plenty of food — but I didn't say: It's a barbecue. Plenty of food, and a reasonable chance of some fun."

Lilia paused for a moment. "I will ask Adena, and if she does not object, we will be there. I will let you know if we are not coming."

"You don't think she will object?"

"No. As I said before: She trusts me."

John had a weird feeling in his stomach as he gave Lilia the details.

After they rang off, he opened a bottle of Locust Mexican and sat in his armchair. "What have I done?" he asked no one in particular.

After a while, John found a baseball game on TV, and Ann snuggled in next to him on the couch.

They woke up at one a.m. to the M*A*S*H theme song.

Monday, July 2

Mason was expecting the regular updates from Eight-ball and Donovan, so when he saw the number on his conspiratorial cell phone, he was surprised.

He was filled with trepidation as he picked up. "Yes?" he asked.

"John, it's Ron."

"I recognized the number, but I wasn't sure it would be you." Mason waited.

"Can't blame you. I want ... I *need* to be part of it again. The unofficial investigation."

"Think so?" Mason was skeptical.

"Look, I know I bailed on you. And you know why."

"I'm sorry I said all of that about Kaiser and —"

Ron cut him off. "Don't go through it again. It's not worth it." Ron inhaled deeply. "And you were right."

"I was?"

"Yeah. Yeah, you were. You were right. I needed to con-front the things that were my fault and realize ... that I *wasn't* responsible for the things that weren't my fault."

Mason sighed. "I suppose you learned all this at church or something."

Ron exhaled a single snicker. "No, not there. I learned it in a hospital waiting room."

Ron couldn't see Mason's eyebrows elevate. "I need to hear more about this."

"Lunch at Chippers?"

"Yeah. One o'clock," Mason said. "I've got to be at the North Fulton Medical Examiner's until then. I can get Don — Wait. You don't know: I brought Donovan and Eight-ball in to see what they can see around the area. I can see if they can come."

"No, don't. Intuition tells me I need to be isolated — you my only contact."

Mason shook his head but agreed.

1:47 p.m.

John and Ron shared a corner table at the back of Chipper's Fish Shack and worked madly to keep the grease off their phones, which sat next to them on the table. Only the strictest mental discipline kept them from fear that the pervasive smell of hot grease would coat their phones irreversibly. Both had two phones because of their recent histories: the detective was wary of being unavailable to his captain; the counselor had promised his family he would stay available. And of course, they had their "unofficial" phones with them.

Ron asked, "Did you hear about Jack Robinson?"

"Robinson? No, why?"

"He had a car wreck Friday. He's badly injured — concussion, back and neck injuries."

"That's some wreck. How'd it ... ?"

Ron inhaled deeply. "He was coming to see me. Apparently, Lenna called because she was worried about me because of how I've treated the family — lots of anger and stressing everyone out. She was right. And Jack was coming to try to talk some sense into me."

"Which started, what, Wednesday? Making me the ... trigger?"

"No. I was ... I don't know how to explain it. Before Wednesday, since the anniversary ..." John knew that Ron meant the anniversary of Barbara's death. "... it's been building up."

John started, "I'm sorry —"

But Ron cut him off. "No! All you did was start me facing squarely the past I was trying to avoid. But the past always comes back, as surely as push always comes to shove. Truly it hurt, but it was like ... removing the dressing from an injury to be able to treat it. The treatment came later, and there's still more required. But ... you did a good thing."

John was slightly weirded out by this, but he understood. "Yeah, the past comes back, like my ex-wife and Adena. I'm having to face up to some of that now."

Ron nodded, but he changed the subject. "I was sorry to hear about your partner. Mark, wasn't it? Last name was Hispanic?"

Mason nodded. "Alcalá, yeah, thanks. He didn't look it though: blond hair; long, thin nose. His great-grandfather or

235

someone came from Spain in the late thirties, escaping Franco, I guess, and moved to Minnesota. Generation after generation married Norwegians.

"I was sitting in on his autopsy this morning. We managed to keep his name out of the news until we could notify his family in Minnesota. That was a tough call to make."

"You made the call?"

"It was me or Captain Berman. I took it because I was working with him daily."

"It wasn't in your jurisdiction, was it?"

"Naw, North Fulton has it. But it's why I was late getting here." Around a bite of fish and hush puppy, Mason asked, "Why did you want to keep the others in the dark about your being involved in ..." He trailed off, waving in the direction of their phones.

"I just felt like independence was a good idea. Besides, I don't move around the city much, so I won't see people the way they will. Why'd you pick them, in particular?"

After a sip of iced tea, Mason said, "They both knew just about everbody at the company. The three of us took the Kaiser stuff to the warehouse when we finally shut down. Our paychecks were the final company business transactions."

Ron took in a forkful of coleslaw, then held up a finger a moment as he chewed. "The warehouse. That break-in coming so soon after Bookman's death made me worry. What if they're related?"

"How could they be related?"

"Did you know about the study contract Book was working on in addition to our project? Very hush-hush, special access clearance."

John's eyes widened. "You knew about that?"

"I had to be read in because he needed to know whether a couple of the algorithms were feasible, meaning could they be implemented to run in less than a century."

"There was a note about it", John said, "*about it*, no content, just a mention — in Bookman's home wall safe. Didn't even give the title. That explains why the guys from FBI counter-intelligence have been hanging around." Mason blinked twice. "Who else had clearance for that?"

"Don't know," Ron said. "Everything I ever saw was Book's handwritten work — some equations and a proof or two and lots of his bad Fortran. It has been a long time ..."

"What was it about? The work, I mean."

Ron's fish halted halfway to his mouth. He whispered, "It was about weaknesses in the standard military encryption."

They sat in silence — the lunch-hour crowd was well and truly done, and there was only one other person in the dining room.

"There's more," Mason said. "Have you heard about the young woman who was killed in Decatur? She was intimately acquainted with Nathan Bookman. You stood next to her at the funeral reception."

"I was sandwiched between two women who made a point of ignoring each other. Was it the tall blonde? Or the brunette?"

"The latter. And it was Mark Alcalá who interviewed her."

It was Ron's eyes' turn to widen. "And now *he's* dead."

They both chewed their final bites and thought for a minute.

"All killed the same way: small caliber gunshot wound."

Ron was opening a packet containing a wet napkin to start trying to clear his fingers of grease. He quoted the old proverb. " 'Two would be a coincidence. Three is a pattern.' What have you learned from Donovan and Eight-ball?"

They both finished cleaning their hands and pocketed their phones. They deposited their used paper goods in to the trash can and trays onto the provided shelf.

"Nothing. I'm sure they've told me everything, but nothing has been useful."

On the way to their cars, John said, "By the way, Ann and I are having a big barbeque for the Fourth on Wednesday. A few people from Kaiser willbe there, plus some cops and some of Ann's employees. You ought to come, and bring the family."

"With major investigations going?"

John shrugged. "My captain insisted, so we're doing it."

"I'll check with everyone. At least one of the kids has something, but I'll check with them. Thanks."

4:06 p.m.

Clarissa's mother, who was originally to have arrived the day after her daughter's surgery to help with recovery, actually managed it the day she went home from the hospital. To Gloria, it seemed that Sarah (who pronounced her own name *SAY-ruh*) and Clarissa were from different worlds. Where Clarissa could be a little abrupt and occasionally swore, Sarah was not just boisterous, but boisterousness itself, constantly fussing and making herself and her care of her daughter unintentionally the subject. At least, it usually *seemed* unintentional.

Ron and Gloria dropped in late in the afternoon, and Sarah offered them coffee. Ron found what she brought them nearly undrinkable. But since he had been raised to know that not only hosts, but guests also, must be gracious, he managed to choke it down a sip at a time.

Sarah was pontificating about Clarissa's now-deceased ex-husband. "I *told* Clarissa that Abe" (she pronounced it Ayeeb) "wasn't any good for her and so when she called I asked if they were *married* and she said no they weren't which was true but she didn't tell me they were *living together* without benefit of a preacher or even a judge. I only found out about that *later* and I was *scandalized*."

Gloria said, "I suppose that when they did get married, it was a relief to you."

"It improved things I sup*pose* and they *did* manage to stay married for a year and a half but then Abe rushed into the arms of someone else and it was *not* unexpected."

"Yes, Mama," Clarissa said. "You have made it clear what you think." Under her breath, she muttered, "You always have."

Ron was the only one who could hear her, since Sarah went on speaking without even acknowledging what Clarissa said.

"I *know* what that was like of course because Clarissa's father *left* when she was only fourteen and I had to raise her sometimes *wondering* where the next week's meals were going to come from because of the expense of raising a child *on my own*."

Ron nodded sympathetically, even as he wondered, *Does she even* know *about commas?*

Conversation proceeded in this vein until Ron mumbled words about overtaxing Clarissa in her recovery.

"I understand," Sarah said as Ron began to open the door for Gloria. "I appreciate the care you have taken of Clarissa and all the food the people from your church brought for someone they don't even know. That's what I kept asking 'how do you know Clarissa?' and everyone said they hadn't met her but her neighbor I guess that was one of you had told them about how she lived alone and would need food that was easy to prepare for at least a few days while she was recovering and it will be good that you are here to help because I couldn't get'ny more time off work and I'll have to go home on Wednesday."

"Of course," Gloria said.

"We'll do everything we can to help," Ron added.

As they crossed the street to go back home, Ron and Gloria both panted with exhaustion.

Tuesday, July 3

7:00 p.m.

Though Mason had sat in on the autopsy, the final report would still be some days in coming. The preliminary M.E. report had no surprises: Mark Alcalá was shot in the head and waterlogged.

The forensics report listed the contents of his pockets, his clothing, the river sediment. And one other item: A small piece of soft, very thin, transparent plastic was lodged in his belt buckle. "Similar to a painter's drop cloth," the report said.

The forensic examination of Alcalá's desk and locker only revealed personal and work possessions; his apartment yielded only the things you'd expect to find in a bachelor's premises. He had a TV, but not an expensive one; his apartment had a land line telephone; there was neither desktop nor laptop computer.

In an attempt to learn who might want to kill Mark, all his background checks for becoming a policeman and then a detective were revisited, and some details were followed up. He had grown up on a farm in rural Minnesota; school and medical records were in order; the Alcalás were still local, having recently sold their farm and moved into the small town nearest. Mason had talked to them while they were packing to come to Atlanta to retrieve their son's body and belongings.

John worried over all these things as he set up the rented tables for tomorrow's picnic. Chairs, still neatly stacked, would wait until tomorrow so dew wouldn't form on them. He loaded the large, rented grill with charcoal, leaving off the lighter fluid until he was almost ready to light it. Ann had already stocked the coolers with beer and soft drinks, and John would go for ice first thing when the store opened.

Last came preparing and loading the big, electric smoker, which would work overnight, since thirty pounds of pork shoulders and about half as much brisket take at least fourteen hours to smoke properly.

With everything in place, he could get a few hours' sleep. An odd memory hit him as he finally drifted off, of his dad telling him about the ice house that *his* father had taken him to just outside their small downtown when he was growing up.

Wednesday, July 4

11:45 a.m.

Everything was set: John had awakened at seven o'clock, and after a quick breakfast and shower, had gone to the store for ice. After icing the drinks, he toweled dew from the tables at Ann's insistence. Around nine o'clock, he had started setting up the chairs in small groups around the periphery of the yard. A light breeze had set in, which would prevent more dew from forming.

When all was done, he looked around, satisfied. The lawn itself was almost flat, with border grasses lining the privacy fence and large flowering bushes of different kinds every few feet. Shade trees — rather, trees that would provide shade in about ten years — were spaced along the southeast side of the yard, framing prize rose bushes, expertly tended and perfectly spaced.

Ann went inside to change from jeans and a work shirt into lightweight navy slacks and a red pullover shirt, and put her dark, armpit-length hair into a white, perfectly bowed hair tie. John didn't change from his khaki cargo shorts and black T-shirt.

The first to arrive at John's barbecue was Henery Guyée — Eight-ball, who wore clean, white painter's pants and a light green golf shirt. He brought two bottles of wine. Ann beamed and greeted him and walked him over to a separate cooler.

"Henery! It's good to see you," Ann said.

"Yes'm, it has been *way* too long. Is there anything I can do to help?"

"Not right now, thanks," Ann said. "John has had the meat on the smoker since last night, and everything else is waiting until time to eat." She spotted three more people coming in through the gate and excused herself.

Eight-ball strolled over to John, who had just finished dousing charcoal with lighter fluid.

"Hey there, Mr Mason."

"Hey," John said. "I wasn't sure you'd be able to make it. And how many times do I have to tell you to call me John?"

"Sorry, the old habit is hard to break. Is there anything I can do to help you?"

"Naw, not right now. In a little bit if you don't mind you can help cook the burgers and brats."

"I'd be happy to. Mrs — Ann, I mean — told me you've been up a while."

"I got a few hours' sleep. It's one of the advantages of using an electric smoker."

"How many folks you expect to come?"

"Around fifty or sixty," John said. "There would have been more, but we weren't sure we'd be able to have the event until the last minute."

Eight-ball looked at the sky. "The weather looks like it

plans to cooperate, anyway."

"Yeah, the forecast has no rain, and the temperature is down about five degrees."

"That's good," Eight-ball said. "Why did you doubt about doing this?"

"We have a big case the department is in all-hands mode for. You may have heard about it — one of our detectives was murdered."

Eight-ball's eyebrows formed a V over his nose, and he frowned. "I heard about that. It's really a shame."

––––––––––––––––––––

Back at the gate, Ann never missed a beat organizing the food and drinks as guests brought them in.

A few off-duty police officers and detectives came bringing various drinks, side dishes, desserts, spouses, and dates. Among the detectives was Michael Renfroe, accompanied by his girlfriend, Constance, a very thin redhead.

In addition to police officers, the staff from Ann's real estate firm all came, as well as a few "others" (as John called them); these last were mostly old employees of Kaiser Transceivers.

In all, about fifty-five people showed up. Predictably, most of the unattached men brought beer or soft drinks or chips or desserts from the grocery store; most of the married and attached brought something they or their partners had cooked or prepared. Oddly (for the South), there was only one gallon of sweet tea.

Ann, predictably, knew the names of forty-two of her guests, even though she had only met about half of them.

"You must have a gardener," someone said to Ann. "Those roses are unbelievable."

"Not a gardener," Ann said, "John grows those. He learned from his mother."

"Really?"

She nodded. "He changed her fertilizer a little, based on new research."

"Does he use pesticides?"

"No, he takes care of pests naturally. If the weather is rainy for more than a day, he'll spray a little fungicide, but other than that he relies on ladybugs and the like."

"That's it?"

"He sometimes sprays for fungus in August —" she waved at someone coming through the gate and started edging that way, "— he says the humidity can be as bad as rain if it goes on long enough. Would you excuse me while I say hello to the Donovans?"

Carlton Donovan and his wife, Mary, and their daughter, Brooks, came through the gate. Carlton wore a Cubs cap to prevent sunburn; Mary wore a green skirt and light beige shirt; Brooks was in yellow shorts and a light blue T-shirt; her hair was the same color as her mom's, but in a French braid rather than a ponytail.

Carlton gravitated to where three-fourths of the men were talking baseball. The other fourth (Michael Renfroe among them) were in a cluster discussing the Major League Soccer season.

Mary found a group of ladies, discovering that most were wives or girlfriends of policemen.

Brooks stood around the periphery of the ladies, near her mom.

A couple of the younger police officers spotted Brooks — which was something of a trick, since she was all of five feet, two inches with a tiny build. When John saw them headed in her direction, he called out, "Askew! Box! Come here a sec."

They altered course and walked over to the grill. The charcoal was almost ready.

John kept his voice low. "I know she's cute, but you need to know she's not even seventeen yet."

Box's eyes widened.

Askew said, "Under age."

"And if that's not enough, her parents are both here."

"Okay," Box said. "But is it a problem to talk to her?"

"No. But like you'd talk to your sister, not like your sister's friend you want to ask out."

Both nodded and walked over to Brooks, slower than they had started.

Two or three of the men and one of the women, all police officers, including Michael Renfroe, joined John at the grill.

Michael stared absently at the charcoal as Catherine Caligari sidled in next to him. She smiled at him and nodded and said, "Detective."

Across the way, someone noticed the grill group and asked, "Who's that next to Detective Renfroe?"

"That's Caligari."

"Really? I guess so ... She's not bad looking when her hair's fixed."

"The lack of body armor helps, too."

"Yeah. Yeah, it does."

"If I were Michael, I'd be noticing *her*."

"The detective has a girlfriend who's here. He's trying to be polite but hold Cal back."

"Ah. So, she doesn't know about the girlfriend."

247

Eight-ball wandered over to where a small klatch of ex-Kaiser employees had gathered. Ron Penfield was among them. Everyone was shifting uneasily, and no one was saying anything.

"Mr Carlton!" he said. "Long time, no see!"

They both grinned. "It has been a while." They hadn't seen each other since two o'clock the previous afternoon. Eight-ball shook hands all around, including Ron's. Ron smiled feebly as he returned the handshake.

"I have to say you all are looking good," Eight-ball said to Carlton. "Who's the young woman who came in with you and Mrs D? Did you get a second wife?" He elbowed Carlton in the ribs.

"That's Brooks, Eight-ball."

"Your daughter? It cannot be!"

"She's almost seventeen."

Eight-ball blinked and stood very still for a moment. He blinked twice and said, "Do you remember Rosa?"

Carlton nodded. "The little Puerto Rican girl?"

"She was seventeen when we met."

"Why did you stop seeing her?"

"Her mama wanted her to marry a good Cath'lic. I wasn't either one," he added with a wink.

"That's one thing her mama and my wife have in common."

Carlton was looking at Brooks, and he didn't see Eight-ball shrug.

Eight-ball's appearance in the Kaiser group had loosened them up a little, and they worked into normal conversation when Ron Penfield left the group to see if he could help with anything near the grill — the folks over there were mostly police officers and wouldn't be uncomfortable around him.

When he was about halfway, he spied a tall, statuesque woman entering the yard, accompanied by a gangly young teenage girl. The woman wore a dark, rose-colored cotton shell with a slit neckline, tailored close but not tight, and a white cotton skirt. Ballerina pumps matched her shirt, and her cheekbones faintly echoed the same color.

She always did overdress a bit, Ron thought.

Through the girl's big glasses, Ron could see her eyes pointed at the ground. Her hair matched her mother's in color but hung limp to her shoulders. She wore a bright green polo shirt, yellow shorts, and blue canvas sneakers.

Ron strolled over to say hello.

"Hello, Lilia. Hello, Adena."

"Hello, Ron. Say hello, Adena." Lilia's voice was deep, her Greek accent voluptuous; her loose, medium brown curls fell to cover her shoulder blades; her eyes were almost the same color as her hair.

Adena's eyes were fixed on Ron's ankles, and she held her hand out at an awkward angle as she said, "Hello. You're Mr Penfield." Her voice was neutral, so flat the pitch hardly varied.

Ron took her hand and smiled. "Yes, I am. It has been a long time — I'm surprised you remember me."

"I remember a lot."

"That you do, dear," Lilia said. To Ron, she offered her condolences on Barbara's death. She also asked about his children; she had met them once at a Christmas party at Kaiser when she and John were still married.

"And Adena," Ron said, "you have become quite the lady."

Adena's eyes flicked up to the face of her mother, who nodded, then back down to Ron's ankles. "Thank you."

Lilia excused herself and her daughter, and as they drifted toward the klatch of former Kaiser employees, many of whom Lilia knew — she and John were divorced after he had been with the company almost three years — Ron muttered, "Lilia's as lovely as ever. And despite her communication problems, Adena doesn't miss much, if anything."

Across the way, Ann noticed Lilia and Adena. As she went to meet them, Ann thought, *She wore a white skirt to a picnic. I bet when she leaves it will still look perfect.*

Reaching them, Ann greeted Lilia and Adena warmly. The wife and the ex had only met a couple of times. Apparently, John had been able to convince Lilia that he really did want to reconnect with his daughter, and that he harbored no malice toward his ex-wife.

Adena and Lilia strolled to the group of former Kaiser employees. Lilia began greeting the people she knew and reintroducing Adena to those. The youngster remembered most of them and greeted them by name. Then she would stand silent as her mother did two-sentence catch-up with each one as they worked their way around the group.

As she did so, Eight-ball was still bending Carlton's ear. "There are a lot of people here," he said. "Do you think this is everyone?"

"There are a few more," Carlton said. "When I was over by the grill, I heard John say that a couple of guys from out of town are coming. He called them 'agents,' but I don't know what kind — maybe real estate agents. Ann's a broker, after all. John said they'd be an hour late, so they must have been showing a commercial property or something."

"Do tell," Eight-ball said, narrowing his eyes.

They both turned as Lilia and Adena worked their way around the group to them. Adena remembered both men.

"Do you still play piano?" Eight-ball asked Adena.

Her eyes rested on his chin. "Yes, sir. I enjoy it."

When the fire on the grill settled down, Eight-ball headed back over to it and began putting burgers and bratwurst on it.

John called Carlton Donovan and Michael Renfroe over, and asked Ron as well, to get the pork shoulders from the smoker and begin separating it with forks — "pulling" it — into foil chafing dishes while John and Eight-ball turned burgers and sausages. Catherine Caligari and Michael's girlfriend, Constance, had finally met and got acquainted as they sliced brisket.

A few folks, mostly women, helped cut buns (French hamburger rolls from Publix, which come uncut), open side dishes (making sure each one had appropriate serving utensils), fill plastic picnic cups with ice, arrange plates at one end of the serving tables, and napkins and utensils at both ends (for those who chronically forgot to get them at the beginning).

Lilia volunteered her assistance to Ann, but Ann held her off.

Ann was possibly the only person present who could say *no* to such an offer and make the offeror grateful. She was not unkind or unfriendly to Lilia — quite the opposite. But as much as she wanted détente between her husband and his first wife, and as much as she wanted warmth between her husband and his daughter, it was still Ann's home. Ann's and John's.

Burgers and brats were starting to come off the grill, and a package or two of hot dogs went on, along with a large pan of marinaded vegetables. Pork shoulders were almost completely pulled, and Caligari and Constance were just about finished slicing brisket.

Mason horse-whistled to get everyone's attention.

"I'm glad you could all come," he called out. "Without getting too syrupy about it we can celebrate freedom because we are free, and because a lot of people, maybe even Mark Alcalá, gave all they had so we could be here."

Everyone nodded. The police officers and detectives nodded with fire in their eyes.

Mason went on. "You guys know Ann and I aren't religious, but I know some of you are. Let's pause for a minute of silence for those who want to pray."

Some bowed their heads, praying or respecting those who did; some waited patiently; one or two waited with bridled annoyance.

"Okay, thanks," John said. "Now Ann will explain the serving rules."

Ann directed people to go down both sides of the tables, and she told them to feel free to sit and rearrange any of the clusters of chairs scattered over the lawn in groups of three and four.

"One last thing," John said. "We originally bought food for a bigger group, but because of the issues we've had, not everyone could come. I'm going to need some of you to volunteer to take away some of the leftovers. Ann and I like barbecue and everything, but there's *way* too much for just the two of us."

Many, especially the single men, greeted this with enthusiasm.

People lined up for food, and then scattered as directed around the lawn to eat.

As serving began, John approached Adena. He sat on the

ground in front of her, making it harder for her to avoid eye contact. They spoke quietly. After a couple of minutes, John stood and took his daughter's hand and led her to look at the roses.

Those who listened as they passed heard John telling Adena about the varieties of roses he cultivated, their individual strengths and weaknesses, blooming schedules, and so on.

When John and Adena finished their garden tour, they got in line. John served her plate and his own as they progressed down the table.

Brooks Donovan and Catherine Caligari took two seats of a set of three and immersed themselves in girl talk. Whenever it looked like a guy or two was going to join them, Cal warned them off with a scowl.

Some, mostly men, went back for seconds, and everyone had a relaxed time talking.

As people began finishing their meals, some of the younger police officers started tossing a football around, and a few of the Kaiser and real estate folks joined in.

Everyone else helped clean up paper goods, cover dishes, and stack about a third of the rented chairs that had been in the center of the lawn.

When cleanup was finished, half of the men were gathered around the grill with John; all the rest were watching a baseball game on the big-screen TV John had moved to the covered porch.

As they gathered, Eight-ball winced and put his hand to his stomach.

"Detective!" someone called to John. "Have you got anything we could use for flags for a football game?"

John said, "Sure." He disappeared into his garage for a minute and came back holding two unopened packages of shop rags, one package of red, the other of blue. He tossed them into the group and said, "Mind the roses."

The group split into two teams and started a disorganized game.

"Are you all right, Eight-ball?" Ron said.

Eight-ball shook his head *no*. Breathing deeply and holding one hand to his stomach, he apologized to John and Ann. "I'm truly sorry to have to go, but I'm not feeling well," he said.

Ann asked, "Can I get you anything to help settle it?"

"No," he said. "I should get home and lie down for the evening."

"I understand," Ann said. "You go home, and I hope you feel better."

He nodded thanks and eased out through the gate, hand still on his stomach.

John went inside.

Lilia and Adena strolled toward Ron.

"I saw your dad showing you the roses," Ron said to Adena. "What did he tell you about them."

Adena began reciting what her father had told her, word for word, until Lilia interrupted. "Adena, dear, Mr Penfield doesn't need every detail, just the main points."

Adena sighed. To Ron she seemed to receive it as a scolding.

"It's okay," Ron said to Lilia as he looked at Adena. "Someone as exceptional as Adena wants to tell everything she remembers."

Lilia looked at Ron with gratitude for understanding.

"Tell me," he went on, "who have you seen here today that you remembered?"

"I saw Mr Dreyfuss who doesn't wear his wedding ring anymore and Mrs Tumblin whose hair used to be brown and Miss Dubé who has a diamond ring and Mr Guyée who started looking concerned when he heard the agents were coming and Mr Spencer with the big circles under his eyes and Mr Ortiz who stared and then looked away and Mrs Locke who gave me a hug."

To Lilia, Ron said, "This is an amazing young woman! You should be proud of her."

"Thank you," Lilia said.

Lilia and Adena drifted toward where Brooks Donovan stood, admiring the roses.

Ron maneuvered through the crowd to the coffee urn behind the grill and dispensed a cup. Holding the cup to upper lip, he inhaled the aroma deeply and blinked a few times.

In a couple of moments, Eight-ball reappeared at the gate and approached Ann.

"Miz Ann, I'm afraid I'm blocked in by two different cars. Can you ask if they can move?"

Ann nodded and said, "Of course. Have a seat and I'll get John to stop the game long enough to get you let out." She went toward the kitchen door, where John was carrying out a bag of ice. After she explained to him that Guyée couldn't leave because of the parking, she continued circulating among the women around the edges of the yard.

John dumped the ice into a cooler, but before he could get everyone's attention, Ron stopped him.

"John, you can't let Eight-ball leave."

"But he's sick. He needs to go home."

"You *can't. Let. Him. Leave.*"

"Why not?"

Ron explained. "He knew Bookman. He knew what was in the warehouse. He was in the warehouse recently, would have seen the security layout. And I think he built a noise suppressor from PVC pipe and washers."

John drew two long breaths and said "Trust me" to Ron. Then he horse-whistled for the game to stop. Everyone around the yard looked at him. "Ya'll take a break for a couple of minutes," he called out. "Can whoever is blocking in the blue and white Duster move your cars to let it out?"

One of the younger officers went to see whose cars were blocking Guyée's in. While they waited, John called Renfroe and Caligari over to him, and he explained to them what they needed to do.

The detective and the officer conferred for a minute, then went back to the waiting football group. They were playing opposite each other: Caligari's team had the ball, and she was wide receiver; Michael played defensive back, as close as these things are counted in flag football.

The owners of the two cars blocking Eight-ball in were both playing ball, but they were on opposing teams, so everyone nodded when Michael suggested they play on.

On the next down, the quarterback was "sacked", moving the line of scrimmage away from the exit where Eight-ball sat waiting.

On the following play, Michael gave his team a bit of extra instruction; Caligari did the same for hers. As they faced each other at the scrimmage line, Renfroe and Caligari nodded simultaneously, then the quarterback got the play going.

Miraculously, no one rushed the quarterback, and from the line Michael hesitated for a second before following Cal as she ran almost the length of the yard. Michael followed on her right. Suddenly they both veered right, and the ball skidded in the grass behind them. Now Renfroe was a step ahead, and they were both heading directly for Eight-ball. Cal swiped the flag from Michael's fanny, Michael swooped his arms around Eight-ball's waist and locked his left wrist in his right hand as Cal stuffed the rag into Eight-ball's mouth.

By this point, everyone was staring. Eight-ball struggled against the hold he was in, but, wiry as he was, Michael held tight, and the action was over.

John trotted over. "Henery True Guyée, you are under arrest for the murder of Nathan Bookman, for the murder of Mark Alcalá, and on suspicion of murder of Ruth Sellers."

When the police officers heard Alcalá's name, they started to press in close. John held up a hand to stop them.

Renfroe called out, "Did anyone bring a patrol car? We need some handcuffs and a ride the station."

Caligari called out "And does anyone know a dentist we can take away from his barbecue?"

"Dentist?" someone in the crowd said. Everyone looked around at the weirdness of the request.

"We need to be able to hold his mouth open."

Grove and Orozco, the FBI agents, walked in at that moment.

Staring at Michael and Guyée, and Caligari hovering over them, Orozco muttered to Grove, "What kind of party *is* this?"

John answered him. "This is the kind where one of us gets to haul his man off to jail. I've got him on two or three murders. I think he's your foreign agent as well."

"The rag in the mouth?" Grove asked.

"I thought he might be old fashioned enough to have a hollow tooth."

257

Grove rolled his eyes. "Urban legend," he said.

Thursday, July 5

"I don't understand, Ron."

Mason and Penfield sat in Ron's home office.

"I want to stay as far away from the spotlight as possible," Ron said. "I want my name and my family kept as far out of it as possible. Farther if you can manage it."

John grimaced. "Only if the prosecutors have to have you."

"That's all I'm asking."

"But why?"

"Because if there's a decent reporter, the whole business with Barbara's murder will get rehashed — and maybe the senator, too — and I'll never have another moment's peace. I just want to lead a quiet life, mind my own business, and make an honest living."

John shook his head. "Some people can do that. But these things seem to come looking for *you*."

They both sipped coffee.

Ron said, "I was surprised to see Lilia and Adena there. Especially without Walter."

"You knew about Walter? Walter's old news," John said. "But yeah, it was weird for me, too. Looks like Adena will be spending some time with Ann and me."

"That's probably a good idea." Ron thought for a second. "Did anything weird turn up in Eight-ball's house? Or his car, maybe?"

"How'd you know?" John asked. "He had a noise suppressor like the one you described. It was held on the front of a small pistol by the front sight. And he had rolls of plastic drop cloth in the trunk of his car."

"So, there wouldn't be residue at the Bookman house."

"A bit of drop cloth was wedged in Mark's belt buckle. And *you* figured out that he wanted to avoid the FBI guys. Speaking of his car trunk, his suitcases were in there, packed, like he was about to do a runner."

"Huh," Ron said. "One way or another, he was saying good-bye."

10:30 a.m.

Later that morning, Clarissa Miller sat with Ron, Gloria, Lenna, Ron Jr, and Ed around the kitchen table as Ron explained what had happened with Guyée. The women were drinking tea; Ron had coffee; Ed had a soft drink.

"It's almost a standard invisible man plot," Ed said. "Even Father Brown had one of those, and that was, like, a hundred years ago."

Clarissa, wide-eyed, leaned toward Ron, who was sitting

directly across from her. "Why do these things happen to you?" she asked, her voice breathy. "It must be exciting."

"It's a little like flying," Ron said. "Hours of boredom are punctuated with moments of terror."

"It's not really boring, is it? Your regular life, I mean."

Ed cut in. "We don't have the most exciting family in the world, but if you're paying attention to all the little stuff, it's never boring."

Ron Jr said, "From the outside it's like watching a base-ball game on TV. But on the inside, it's like being at the ball park and seeing that there's always something going on some-where. The way all the pieces fit together — the motions of a base coach while a batter is warming up, signals given to the catcher to give to the pitcher, a hundred little things — it's more interesting than exciting."

"I need to learn more about all that," Clarissa said. "My husband taught me to love hockey, but it's very different: All the action is right there in front of you on the ice."

Everyone nodded.

Clarissa looked at Ed. "What did you mean by 'invisible man'?"

"An invisible man — it could be a woman, it's just a name — is someone you ignore because he's *supposed* to be there. In the Father Brown story, it was a mailman."

"I see," Clarissa said. "Well, I guess I should be going. I need to get some rest."

Everyone said goodbye, and Clarissa left through the garage.

As the door shut, Gloria and Lenna crossed their arms si-multaneously and stared at Ron. Lenna's head tilted the way Barbara's used to.

He looked back and forth at them. "What?"

"Really, Ron." Gloria said.

"Do you have to ask, Daddy?"

Ed said, "Huh?" and looked back and forth between the women.

Ron blinked several times. "Oh," he said. "Oh!"

Ron Jr nodded.

Ron sprinted out the door and caught up with Clarissa halfway across the street.

"Um, I was wondering ..." He gulped a couple of deep breaths — he was unaccustomed to running.

Clarissa's eyes opened wider, and a faint smile crept across her lips.

"After you've rested, would you like to go to dinner tonight?"

Her smile broadened and deepened. "I'd love to!"

8:30 p.m.

At home that night, John and Ann were eating leftovers from the barbeque.

"So Henery Guyée was a spy?" Ann asked. "For whom?"

"Belarus. One part of the old Soviet bloc that's still chilly from the Cold War."

"Was he looking for anything in particular?"

John described the paper on decryption math Nathan Bookman had written. "Apparently Bookman told someone about the paper in an unguarded moment. Maybe he had too much to drink. We won't know about that now, unless Eight-ball tells us."

"Decryption," Ann said. "Very cloak-and-dagger stuff."

"On a battlefield, with a big enough computer, a hostile army could intercept transmissions and decrypt them in real time."

"And with computers getting faster, smaller, and cheaper all the time ..."

"Exactly — Moore's Law. That new phone Apple announced has more computing power than a second-generation PC. And if you can't get the hardware to do this today, you can do it next year or the year after."

"How was your junior detective involved?"

"Alcalá? I can only guess."

"So, guess."

John drew a breath. "Try this out: Mark was from up north someplace. Minnesota, I think. Suppose that was just a cover story, and he was really another agent."

"For Belarus, like Guyée?"

"Mm hmm. He told me at one point that he was interested in dating the woman, Ruth Sellers."

"The brunette who was involved with Bookman?"

"Yep. If Mark found out she knew something from her association with Bookman, he'd tell his handler, who *might* have been Guyée, and the dominoes would be set to fall. If she became a risk — she might have seen the handler and be able to recognize him, say — that would put her life in danger."

"Poor girl. How did she get attached to Bookman?"

"She worked at a bar in Buckhead he went in sometimes. She was looking for love —"

"Don't say it!" Ann cut in. She shook her head. "Someone should have told her that you don't turn counterfeit money into real money by giving it away." She took a bite of her sandwich

263

and chewed. "And Mark himself?"

"He was young. If he had any kind of feelings for her, puppy love, or even just regret about killing her — whoever did it — that made *him* a risk."

Ann considered her sandwich for a moment. "This is about best you've ever done on the smoker."

Had John's smile not been from honest humility, it would have been considered a smirk. "Thanks."

"But ..." he trailed off.

"Yes?"

"They almost got away with it — the killings anyway. The FBI guys wouldn't say they recovered Bookman's paper from the warehouse, but there would be a lot more activity if they hadn't, so the country's secrets are safe."

"How did they almost get away with it? Wasn't there enough evidence to get to them?"

"No," John said. "Eight-ball knew how to cover his tracks. Essentially, he took all the evidence away with him, bundled up in a painter's drop cloth."

Ann gazed at her sandwich. "You mean there was no trace?"

Acknowledgements

Many thanks go to my beta readers, Andrew Crigler, Alyssa Catalano, and Paula Lowder. Your contributions made this a much stronger book.

And Jennie: Your constant love and encouragement helped me refuse to quit.

Dedication

To Terry Eugene Huey. I know you wanted to be a serial killer, but spy and assassin will have to do. NB: Next time you are born, ask your parents to give you a name with fewer "U"s.

www.ingramcontent.com/pod-product-compliance
Lightning Source LLC
Chambersburg PA
CBHW031708170626
46808CB00005B/1665